# I NEVER Asked YOU To SAVE Me

Book 4

The Wakefield Romance Series

Theresa Marguerite
Hewitt

Copyright © 2013 Theresa Marguerite Hewitt

All rights reserved. No part of this may be reproduced or transmitted in any form or by any means without written permission from the author.

Edited by Genevieve Scholl

Cover design by Najla Qamber Designs

ISBN: **149497519X**
ISBN-13: **978-1494975197**

# DEDICATION

To my family:

Thank you for letting me chase this dream. This is for
Jerry Jr. If you were still with us, I'd hope you'd be
proud of your little sis. I love you.

**"What you think could be the end, may very well
be only the beginning."**

# CONTENTS

# ACKNOWLEDGMENTS

To My Readers:
Thank You!
I can never say it enough. From those who enjoy my Facebook posts and give me non-stop encouragement, to those who follow my blog and YouTube; I will never be able to show you all of my gratitude. Your support through my learning journey is what makes me a better writer and person over all.

# CHAPTER 1

*Ellie*

*February 14, 2013*

"It's too freaking early," I groan to myself as I silence the alarm on my phone and rub my eyes. I silently curse myself for the simple action as pain shoots up into my skull. I have to bite my lip to hold in a slight scream. Angrily throwing my legs over the side of my twin bed, I utter, "Damn you Jake," under my breath and shuffle my way into the bathroom.

Seeing my bruised cheek and the broken blood vessels in my right eye looking back at me from the mirror makes me angry. I told myself I'd never let him hit me again, but I hadn't been expecting him to be outside my trailer when I got home from working at the club last night. "My momma didn't raise me to be weak," I whisper to myself while cranking on the faucet to try and wash away the tear and sleep streaked makeup.

That's right. My mother, Ellen Griggs, hadn't raised me to be like this. After sweeping me and my older brother Jack up without warning when I was two and he was four and moving us from our little town of Wakefield, she had always told me to be a strong woman and not to take any shit. I've utterly failed her in that notion.

After shoving Jack and I into a beat up Honda in the middle of the night, my mom trucked us to my aunt's house in Tennessee. My father, Rick, was a horrible man, but don't you know it, to this day I can't remember what he looks like or what his voice sounded like. It's a good thing, I guess, since he left my mother with a huge scar across her cheek. She rarely ever spoke of him when Jack and I were growing up, moving around so many times I can't remember half. We lived with my aunt just outside of Nashville until I was six, then bounced around from California, Las Vegas, Colorado, and small towns in between; finally settling in Lewisburg, West Virginia, just off of I-64 in sight of the Blue Ridge Mountains.

I had a good childhood and I can't help but smile as I think of walking to school on the nice days, with Jack and his football buddies tagging along in front of me and my dance friends. Jack was the best big brother any girl could ask for. He made sure none of his friends bothered me too much and that I was doing well in class and on the sports teams. My mom was happy, working in a local bank, and she provided us with everything that she could, including dance lessons for me four nights a week.

I love dance—or I should say, *loved dance*, because I haven't put on a pair of pointe shoes in almost four years. I was trained in ballet, tap, jazz, hip-hop, and contemporary. Ballet was my strong point and the tattoo of purple pointe shoes in the middle of my back pays homage to it. Since I was four, I had wanted to be a ballerina, dancing for a crowd somewhere like Broadway or Moscow. My mom and Jack had encouraged me the entire way, and when I was sixteen I was accepted into the West Virginia Dance Academy, a high end dance school led by a former Russian ballet star. Sixteen was my down-fall age, however, because that's when I met Jake.

Jake Heart was the typical high school heart throb that every girl wanted to be with; blonde, blue eyed with muscles that seemed to go on for days, but he had picked little cheerleader me, short, curvy with dark almost black hair and blue-green eyes, when I was a Junior and he was a Senior. I guess you could have called us the 'it' couple, being everywhere that anything cool was happening. He asked me to marry him the day of his graduation and I was head over heels for him, so I said yes. He was a County Sheriff by the time I was a senior, supposedly establishing a career and building a life for the two of us.

My senior year brought Jack enlisting in the Marines and shipping off, leaving me and my mom to our happy little world. He called and wrote, visiting on leave every so often, but then Mom was diagnosed with liver cancer. She battled with all she had, but it was too advanced. She got to see me graduate with high honors and get accepted into the Dance Program at West Virginia Wesleyan College, and then walk down the aisle with Jack escorting me in full uniform. She died three weeks after my wedding to Jake, going peacefully in her sleep and leaving a huge hole in my heart.

That's when everything went downhill. After the funeral, Jack went back to his base and barely called, emailed, or wrote. I haven't heard from him in a year, and I worry about him every day. I was packed and ready to go off to college after selling my mother's house, but was stopped when Jake protested. It was the first time he hit me, and it was one of the worst to date. In the small trailer he had bought for us, he yelled and screamed, fueled by beer and liquor, striking me across the face and knocking me down, scaring the living hell out of me.

He profusely apologized, saying he'd never do it again, that cliché abuser line, but as soon as the words "I'm leaving, I need to be at school tomorrow," came over my lips, he snapped. He pushed me down and brought his steel toed boot down on my ankle so hard, it shattered and I blacked out, waking up in the ER hours later. Two pins and three hours of surgery later, when the doctors were out of the room, Jake apologized again, showering me in flowers and getting me to tell the Doctors and police that I had fallen down the porch steps. It's one lie I wish I could take back to this day.

I had to drop out of school, because no one wanted a damaged ballerina, and had gone to night school under the watchful eye of my husband, gaining an Associate's Degree in Office Management. He drank and partied, acting the part of the dutiful husband when we were out and about. But at home, as soon as the door was shut and locked, he was another person. He seemed to get off on the pain that he caused me, being a fan of overzealous hair pulling, spanking, and even choking. I became a pro at using cover up and sunglasses to hide the evidence, having only his partner's wife, Yolanda Walden, to confide in as she suffered abuse at the hands of her husband, Tom, as well.

Why did I stay? I stayed because he is a cop. He can find me whenever and where ever. He always threatened that if I left he'd hunt me down like a dog and make it ten times worse than before. My little temp jobs in legal offices kept me desensitized to everything wrong in my life, but in June everything looked up for once. I found out I was pregnant and I was overjoyed.

I had planned a special dinner, getting Jake's favorite steak and lobster and preparing it just the way he liked it and waiting for him to come home from his shift. I had on the dress he loved and had done my hair, ready to share with him the happy news. Standing as the door opened, I was smiling wide, with my hands never leaving my stomach, but the look in his eyes changed my feelings into fear instantly. Without a word, he backhanded me as I tried to escape to the bedroom, screaming at me that I was worthless.

I yelled and cried, "Jake no," but he didn't let up. After what was only seconds, but seemed like hours, I screamed that I was pregnant and he froze, pinning my arms down by my head on the hallway floor. I struggled against his hold, the chains of his abuse holding me here, holding me to Jake, finally shattered in my heart. I wasn't going to take this anymore, especially not now. The look on his face softened as he professed his love to me, kissing me hard and forcing me to have sex with him right there and then as I cried and protested, but every time I would say no, he would just kiss me, silencing it to a mumble.

As he was passed out on the bed, the food still on the table, I felt sick to my stomach. Stripping and throwing that damn black dress in the garbage, I put on sweatpants and other comfortable clothes, dressing for the abnormally crisp summer night. Tossing underwear and essentials into a tote bag, I grabbed what cash I could find and left, not looking back. I ran, not caring that the roads were dark or that only hours ago I was actually happy to be carrying his child. I just ran. Seven miles later, I reached the closest bus station, collapsing in tears on a bench and calling a co-worker from one of my temp jobs.

I wanted to go home. I wanted to go back to Wakefield. My childhood memories brought back smiles as I cried to her on the phone and she agreed to come get me and take me to a friend of hers, Marco Patuli, who would help me out. She drove me all through the night, crossing the state line into Virginia and finally making it to the little town of Waverly around sunrise. We pulled up at the back door of Subzero Strip Club, and she left me with a hug and kiss, telling me to call if I needed her, but I haven't. Marco has been an angel.

Marco is a thirty something entrepreneur, who owns four clubs in Virginia and one in Las Vegas. That first day he came out the back door of his club in a silk dress shirt with rolled up his sleeves and unbuttoned enough to let his chiseled chest peek out, a wide caring smile on his face. He always keeps his hair short and tousled, kind of like his choice in men, which he has many of at any time. As soon as he saw me with the tears rolling down my cheeks his dark brown eyes softened and his brow furrowed, throwing his arm around my shoulders and ushering me inside the club and into his office. He has money and friends and within the first couple of hours, I was set up in a rented trailer in Waverly, neighbors to a couple of his employees. I also had an interview for a temp job at the Sussex county DA's office the next week, which I got. He even fronted me three hundred dollars to buy a car.

The loud playback of Jason Aldean's "The Only Way I Know" snaps me out of my musing and with a hard scrape of a towel across my face, wiping away the makeup and tears, I swipe my phones screen and put it up to my ear, knowing it's my cousin Rhea. "It's only six in the mornin'; why aren't you still sleeping?" I grumble into the receiver while trying to pull on a pair of Nike jogging capris to go for my morning run.

"Well hello to you, too, Ellie," she torts, laughing lightly. She had been through a tremendous amount of shit in the last six months and I'm glad we've found each other. I never expected to have any family left in Wakefield and was surprised when I read the announcement for her baby shower in the local paper during the summer. She's been a beacon of strength for me.

"First off, happy birthday!" She all about squeals and I inwardly groan, not wanting to remember that today is my twenty-third birthday. She giggles and continues, "I was just up with Charlie and wanted to make sure you're still comin' tonight?" she asks and I can just imagine the little sly grin on her lips. Tonight was a "Come Home Soon" party she and her husband Chad were throwing for his old SEAL teammates who are deploying in a day and a half, and Rhea is still trying to kind of set me up with Bobby Timmons.

It's not too hard because the man is gorgeous. Tall, muscular, with dirty blonde hair and light freckles across his cheeks. His hazel eyes can cut right through me every time I see him and just the thought of him makes my heart flutter even now with the bruises throbbing on my face, but I can't do it yet. I can't drag someone into this hell that I call a life until I get rid of Jake for good.

"Yeah I'm still comin', Ray-Ray," I tease, turning the speaker on as I pull on a sports bra and tank, tying my short hair up in a knobby ponytail and fixing the fly-away and loose ends with bobby pins.

"Okay." She giggles and I can hear little Charlie happily gurgle in the background, making me laugh along with her. "I'll see you around four then, after you drop off some things at your new trailer, right?"

"Yeah, I'll text you when I'm headed over," I reply, saying goodbye as I tie up my sneakers, standing to stretch a little as I cue up my IPod. I had been planning to move into a trailer in the park closer to Rhea for the last two weeks and have my sparse belongings already packed into the back of my beat up Chevy Beretta. It makes me even more pissed that Jake found me right on the verge of me being finally happy.

I had felt like I was away from him for good. The DA I temp for, Paul Jesop, had served Jake with the divorce papers and now it was time to just wait for him to sign them. Even though Rhea and Chad have asked me a million times to move in with them, I've refused because I want to make it on my own and this trailer was going to be it. I had put my first three months down in cash that I had earned on my temp jobs and moonlighting at Subzero.

Yes, I work at a strip club. Yes, I dance, but Subzero isn't some sleazy place you go to get a 'happy ending' after work. There is a dress code for patrons, and dances are not cheap. Plus, I always wear wigs and little masquerade masks when I'm on stage and either Marco or one of his bouncers screen the guys who ask for me. They check ID's and keep watchful eyes on all the guys. And it's just plain fun. It's a total power trip when you're up there with all eyes on you. It lets me unwind and forget about my problems.

It's the same as running, and as I plug my ears with the bud speakers and strap my iPod onto my arm, zipping up my red track jacket, I'm out the door, jamming out to Kelly Clarkson. I wave to two of my co-workers from the club, Melody and Shae, as I pass by where they are seated on Melody's porch. I can see their eyes go right to my face as they smile and wave, and I angle it away, picking up my pace to get away from them while trying to tell myself it's to stay off the chill in the air. Turning right out onto the county road, I zone out to Kelly blaring away in my ears that what doesn't kill you, makes you stronger. I beg to differ.

Pushing the dark thoughts out of my head, I focus on the road in front of me. The wet, soggy grass and the crunching gravel under my feet as I wave at the familiar cars and trucks that honk, coming to and fro from the trailer park. My breathing is even and steaming around my face as I hesitate at a stop sign, making sure someone isn't going to come screaming around the corner and run me over. I keep on, heading toward one of my favorite spots.

About three miles away from the trailer park and right on the town lines for Waverly and Wakefield is a horse farm. Springtime Equine Barn is the name and it sprawls over more than twenty acres. Slowing my pace, I look for my favorite horse. She is a spirited Champagne with a light tan coat and darker brown mane. Over the last few months it became more evident to me that she is going to have a foal, but every day without fail, she'll see me and come to the fence line, letting me scratch her nose and talk to her.

But today, I don't see her. I see all of her usual companions, but not *my* horse. Slowing to an even jog, I turn into the dirt driveway to the main house, running in place and looking around for the familiar farmers as ACDC powers onto my iPod. I have used their driveway for a turn around since I started taking this path and I've come to know Kelley Spring and his wife, Gertrude, enough to carry on a polite conversation in the local grocery. They have three boys, and as I go to turn back toward home, I see the youngest, Bryan, emerge from the closest barn and he waves.

"Hey guy," I yell, taking my ear buds out and

10

heading over to him. He is about ten, skinny and lanky with messy blonde hair and his smile is wide as ever as I make it to him. "Where's Lady?" I ask, looking around him and seeing his father approach with a wink.

"Hey Ellie." Kelley waves, whipping a towel over his shoulder and adjusting the worn out cap on his head. He slaps a massive, hard-worked hand on Bryan's shoulder. "Go in and tell your momma to make breakfast," he whispers in the boy's ear, and he goes running after telling me to have a good day. Turning back to Kelley after watching his boy run into the large farmhouse, I see the strained look on his brow.

"What's wrong, Kel?" I query, following close behind him as he waves over his shoulder for me to come into the warm barn. The smell of musty hay and manure meet me, but don't bother me. I've always wanted to live on a farm, and would love to own some horses. I keep quiet, weaving around the stalls as Kelley scrapes his hand back through his short blonde hair again, stopping by the open door of one and my eyes go up to the sign stating "Lady" with curly lettering.

"She started to foal last night." His thick country accent flows around me as I step forward with wide eyes. The normally full of life mare is laying on her side, her rib cage rising and falling in rapid succession. Looking back and seeing the grim look on his face, Kelley says, "The foal died about two hours ago, and I can't get her to get up."

I take in a sharp breath as the familiar pain fills my heart and my hands go to my abdomen as tears fight to line my lashes. Looking back to the horse, I grind out, "Is there anything wrong with her, or is she just distraught?" I let the last word linger on my lips as I re-live my own pain, sitting curled up in a ball on my bed or couch, crying until there are no more tears to be shed. The only difference, my pain had been self-inflicted; I had done it to myself because I had seen no other way. I hadn't seen any good for anyone coming from it.

"Yeah, she just dropped down after Bryan took the body out. Almost crushed my leg." He tries to smile, but I can see the stress lines on his forehead. We just stand there, not saying anything as my heart is silently breaking for the struggling mare. She is broken, like me. She is scarred, like me. I am zoned out when Kelley's hand touches my shoulder, scaring me. "I'm not sure I can do anythin' for her if she won't get up on her own. Why don't you see if you can get her up?"

His eyes seem to cut right through me, searching for something as he looks at me. It's like he can tell I know how she feels, but how could he? His fingers squeeze my shoulder lightly as he tries to smile, and I nod.

"What about the vet?" I almost squeak, looking from Kelley to Lady with fast glances, trying not to let the pain flooding my heart topple over and become visible on the outside. No one knows what I chose to do. No one is ever going to know.

"I don't have any money to pay the vet 'cause I still owe her a thousand dollars for the last birthing. She said she'd come if I need her, but I don't want to waste the call and the money, you know?" He is a struggling farmer and family man, and I can totally understand his stand on not wasting money.

I take a deep breath in, rubbing my hands on my thighs and take a few hesitant steps forward into the hay covered stall. She doesn't even flinch as I round her face, but her eyes watch me and I can see the same sorrow in her as I see in me. Kneeling down in front of her front legs, with my knees close to her chest, I slowly, carefully run my hands down her neck, feeling the muscles twitch. She lifts her head for a second, her eye peering at me as if she is telling me to go away. As she lays it back down, I lean my forehead down on her neck, running my fingers through her wiry mane.

"I know it hurts, girl," I whisper, fighting those tears away from my lashes, "but you gotta get up. You gotta keep goin' or it's not gonna end well for ya." As I lift my head, she huffs out a breath, sending a cloud of dust up around her face and she throws her head up, almost knocking me over.

Kelley steps in front of me, coaching Lady to her feet. "Come on, girl," he encourages gruffly, reaching one hand out to me that I take so he can pull me up as Lady gets to her feet, shaking her coat of the hay and dirt. "Alright," he smiles, running his hand over her shoulder and down to her hip, patting it as Lady whinnies lightly.

"I don't know what you said, but thank you." He grins, shaking my hand as I shake my head, trying to play it off as I didn't do anything. Like I don't know what the horse is feeling.

As he checks her out, I step outside the stall, falling back against the rough wood, leaning my head back and closing my eyes. "*You made the right choice*," I tell myself silently as my hands grip into my track jacket, my knuckles turning white, and "*what kind of life would they have had? With a father that would beat them like he beat you? But you have Rhea; she would've helped you."* That voice of guilt always sneaks its way into things when I try and talk myself out of a breakdown, but the slamming of the stall door brings me out of it, facing a still smiling Kelley.

"I don't know what ya did, Ellie, but she seems to be doin' okay now." He grins, placing his hand on my shoulder as he leads me out of the barn. He's chatting away, but I'm not listening. My mind is still trying to put itself back together. As my eyes roam over the wet gravel and the few puddles near the door, a light pat on my shoulder pulls me out of it. Shaking my head at him, telling him I didn't hear what he said, makes him laugh. "I said, did you wanna come in for some breakfast?"

"Oh, no thank you." I smile, patting him politely on the arm before backing away down the driveway, putting in one of my ear buds and cueing up my ACDC again. "I gotta get home. Today's movin' day remember!?" I smile and wave before turning around after Kelley does the same. Then I take off, trying to shake off the pain from my heart as I push my legs harder and faster than before.

Pushing my legs until it feels like they aren't even touching the ground, the pavement passes by under my feet as the grass, trees, and the far between houses fly by, but I'm not really paying attention. The tears had started as soon as I turned out of the Springs' driveway and they flow down my cheeks as my heart tries to put itself together. *"I had to do it,"* I tell myself, *"I couldn't be a mother to a child when I couldn't even take care of myself."* Hesitating for only a split second at the stop sign, I sprint across the road and keep up the pace, wanting to get to my car and leave for my new trailer in Wakefield.

I want to leave all this pain behind, but it never leaves. It's attached to me like a shadow. It will seem like it has disappeared, but then when I least expect it, it rears its ugly little head and breaks me down, again.

As I turn into the familiar rows of trailers, I see the fancy, shiny, brand new Audi R8 parked in front of my soon to be former home, with Marco's stocky, well defined figure leaning against the back of it, talking with Melody. Their gazes hit me as I start to slow up, turning down the volume of Luke Bryan on my iPod and popping one of the ear buds out. I really don't want to talk right now, to anyone. I just want to get in my shitty Berretta and get to my new trailer, put my stuff away, and take a long, hot shower.

"Well, look who decided to finally come back." Marco smiles, flashing his perfectly straight, white teeth; and I can't help but shake my head and grin, stopping and trying to catch my breath. I lean my hip on the taillight of his grossly expensive car as I feel his dark eyes roam over me, hesitating on my right cheek and eye; a deep crease forming in his brow.

"Yeah, well, I'm gonna go get to bed." Melody looks me over, giving me a sad sort of smile as she notices the bruise, throwing her arm out for a one armed hug. She is taller, maybe five foot eight, with light mocha toned skin and bright pink, curly hair. She is one of the sweetest girls that work at the club with me and we have gotten close. She has two little girls, one seven and one four, with no father in the picture, and she works hard to make sure they want for nothing. "I'll miss havin' ya so close, Ell," she says, giving me a pout before releasing me.

"I know, but we'll see each other almost every night anyway." I grin, shrugging my shoulders, and she giggles, kissing Marco on the cheek like usual before jogging over to her trailer and disappearing. Turning my attention back to my boss, I see his thick, muscular arms crossed over his chest and an eyebrow cocked, looking at me with a sidelong glance.

Shoving his attention off, I jog up the short set of stairs, throwing the door open to go and gather the last couple things from the bathroom and bedroom. The door slams behind me and I whirl around to face the intense gaze, being only a few inches from my face. His fingers grip my chin, rotating it until my bruise is right in his line of sight and I strain my eyes to see him.

"Why didn't you call me?" he whispers, his voice husky and deep as he releases my chin, his hands moving to my shoulders and gripping them gently. I can't look at him, but I can feel the concern in his attitude. I don't want to talk about last night, I just want to get to my new home, so I shake my head and Marco sighs deeply, releasing me to go grab my things.

As I'm gathering the blanket and pillow from the bed, I see him from the corner of my eye lean on the doorway, his hands shoved in the pockets of his designer jeans. "You know why I go out of my way to help you, Ellie?" he mutters and I turn on him.

"You mean it's not my bubbly personality and impeccable looks?" I joke, trying to give him a mischievous grin as I shove my things into his arms. I flick my fingers through my short hair and he snorts, following me into the bathroom.

"My dad beat my mom." He sighs and I stop what

16

I'm doing, turning to look at him with a slight shock on my face. Why was he telling me this? "I see her in you." He tries to give me a smile, but I can still see the pain behind it and it makes me feel guilty. It makes me feel weak.

Throwing the face wash and makeup into a plastic grocery bag, I turn and get up on my tip toes, kissing him lightly on the cheek. "I don't need you to worry about me," I whisper, running my hand over his tense shoulder and chest. "I can take care of myself."

"That bruise begs to differ," he snaps, snorting at me as he turns and stomps back into the kitchen/living area. Slowly following behind him, I'm scanning the area to make sure I'm not leaving anything behind when I bump right into his chest, turning my shocked face up to see his very serious one. "You call me next time. No matter what time it is."

His eyes go from hard to soft in a split second, trying to burrow his message into me and I grin up at him, nodding my head. Even though Marco is interested in men most of the time, I've seen him woo women off their feet in seconds just by looking at them, and right at this moment, I can see why. His eyes are a chocolate brown, framed by prefect lashes on his strong featured face.

I hit him lightly in the chest and have to drag my gaze away from his with a blush. "Okay, okay I'll call you," I give in and he thanks me. "Never give me the Marco stare ever again," I warn and he chuckles, wrapping me in a hug from behind. He pokes and prods me until we're out in the driveway, throwing the last things into the passenger seat of my car.

"I'll follow you." He smiles, sliding into the

driver's seat of his tuned up sports car and pushing on his sunglasses with exaggerated movements. I can't help but roll my eyes, slamming the door shut on my Beretta and bringing her to life. She's loud, but she runs well and I crank up the radio, blaring Eric Church as I whip it backward and spray gravel at Marco. He throws his hands up and honks his horn as I mouth an "Oops" to him with a grin, flooring it out of the trailer park and screeching my tires on the pavement of the road; headed toward my new home in Wakefield.

Fifteen minutes later, we pull into the Wakefield trailer park, passing that bastard Duke Orr's old trailer, now occupied by his cousin Jesse Ludwell. I curse under my breath, hoping he's having a horrible time in jail. Two more down, we come to mine. The outside is a light rust kind of color with dark brown shutters. Pulling into the gravel covered, one car drive, I park my Beretta close to the porch to make it easy to unload my boxes, and Marco revs his engine, pulling behind me.

I shake my head and wag my finger at him as he grins, revving the engine again, letting the turbo whine and then shutting it off. "You'll make enemies with my neighbors," I chide, running up the steps and unlocking the screen and storm doors, propping them open.

The inside isn't the best, but it is mine for now. The carpet is thin and brown all throughout the single wide; minus the kitchen and bathroom, which are cheap beige linoleum. The walls are faded, peeling floral wallpaper, which I plan on re-painting when I have the cash. I can hear Marco's grumbles and disapprovals as he carries the first couple of boxes in.

"Wood paneling." He smirks, setting the boxes down in the living room, tapping his fingers on the hallway paneling that looks like it's straight out of the seventies. "Classy," he mumbles and I hit him on the shoulder, pushing him back out the door to get more boxes.

I want to get this unloading and some unpacking done so I can take a shower. I need to wash away the events of last night and this morning.

Plus, I get to see Bobby in a few hours and he always makes me feel good.

# CHAPTER 2

*Ellie*

I've been laying on the mattress in my new bedroom for an hour now, wrapped only in a towel after flopping down here right out of the shower. The ceiling is yellowed but it's starting to be less visible as the shadows of the moving sun bring the afternoon. Marco left when all the boxes were in from my car, needing to attend a meeting at his newest project in Virginia Beach.

I've been laying here replaying the confrontation with Jake from last night, unable to get the anger in his face out of my mind. *"Where's the baby, you whore?"*

he had yelled, grabbing my arms as I threw them up to try and protect myself, yanking me to him and holding me tight as he screamed in my face. *"Did you kill our baby? You're a no good piece of shit; you're a baby killer,"* he spat, pushing me back and slapping me the first time, knocking me to my knees.

His words stung harder than his hit and even now, lying on my back alone in my empty trailer, they bring tears to my eyes. I hadn't said anything in reply to Jake's name calling; I had kept my mouth shut, taking the physical and emotional blows like I always had and trying to file them away so they won't crack the wall around my heart. He had pulled me to my feet, his nose bumping mine as he growled more insults at me, shaking me as he screamed, *"Why would you do that to me? To our baby?"* Then he had let it loose, hitting me until I was nothing but a crying, curled up bundle in the middle of the living room floor, leaving with the slam of the front door.

"I did it because there would have come the day when the child would have pissed you off about something, and you would have hit them," I whisper to myself, sitting up and letting the towel fall away. "You would have hit them and then I would have to kill you." It is the truth. Jake could have sworn up and down that he would never hit the child like he did me, but it was all lies and when that day came, I wouldn't be able to take it. I did what I did to spare the child from a life of pain and torment.

Three loud knocks make me jump and I stand frozen for a second, my heart beating a mile a minute in my ears. Maybe I am hearing things, but no, three loud knocks again and I yell, "Hold on a minute," hurriedly searching in my duffle bags, pulling on a bra and panty set. The knocks come again, this time louder as I'm stumbling down the wood paneled hallway tugging on a pair of jeans, a red tank, and a striped, hooded thermal.

Reaching the front door, I grip the handle and yank it open, angrily saying, "I said I was comin'," when the man on the steps catches my eye. It is Jude Faber, a bouncer from Subzero, standing in a tight muscle revealing tee and worn out, snug jeans with a killer grin on his lips. "H-hey," I stammer, subconsciously running my fingers through my still damp, bobbed hair, brushing it back off my forehead.

"Hey Ellie." He grins, shoving his hands into the front pockets of his jeans and making my eyes skip over their position and notice the bulge in the blue jean material. "Jus' wanted to say welcome to the neighborhood." I'm still kind of speechless as I grunt a reply, leaning on the doorway and taking in the handsome man's appearance.

Jude is about five foot ten; tan and a work-out junkie, the bulging muscles under his shirt atone to that. A few of his numerous tattoos peek out from under the collar of his shirt and at the openings of his sleeves. I snap out of it, noticing that I'm making him a little nervous as I ogle him and he runs his hand back through his short, gel spiked black hair, his light brown eyes darting from me to his feet.

"Oh, yeah, thanks," I smile, "did you wanna come in?" I side step, waving my hand for him to come in and he chuckles, nodding his head and walking past me. Shutting the door, I turn to see him appraising the boxes of my stuff and the worn out furniture supplied by the landlord. "I haven't had time to unpack much, but I might have a few beers

22

somewhere. Would you like one if I can find them?"

"Yeah." He grins as I frantically look through the plastic grocery bags containing what was left in my fridge at the old trailer. "Marco stopped by before he left and said you had just moved in so I figured I'd give you a couple of hours before sayin' hello." He has a nice melodic voice, and I nod my head to him as I keep rummaging through the bags, finally coming to a box and spotting the bottles.

"Got'em," I say triumphantly, and Jude laughs as I hold the bottles up. Feeling that the bottles are not too warm, I hand him one with a smile. He quickly twists off the cap, reaching over and doing the same to mine as he puts his to his lips. "Well, this is it." I giggle clearing a spot for him to sit on the couch.

"Well, I'll help ya unpack if ya want," he says, wiping the back of his hand across his mouth. I really don't have that much stuff, but the help would be nice so I nod, pointing him to the boxes piled in the corner of the kitchen.

"That would be mighty nice." I pinch him on the shoulder, taking a swig of my beer. "If you wanna tackle the kitchen, I can get my clothes and bathroom stuff put away before gettin' to my cousin's house." He grins and turns, trotting into the kitchen as I go back into the bedroom, flicking on all the lights to make sure they all work.

"What you got goin' on at your cousin's?" he yells as I can hear him going through the plastic bags and the fridge door opening and closing.

Turning one of my duffle bags upside down on the full sized mattress, I start to sort through my clothing; pulling open the drawers on the ancient oak dresser. "There's a party for some friends," I reply, hearing the clang of pots and pans going on out there. I barely hear the mumbled reply and we settle into unpacking. I turn on the radio plugged into the hallway socket and crank up the local rock station, seeing a smile from Jude over the counter island.

I'm zoned out, singing along with Halestorm when I turn into Jude's chest, his arms going around my shoulders to steady me. "Sorry, but I'm all done out there," he says over the music with a grin and I nod for him to help me hang things, tossing him some plastic hangers from the small closet. He hangs and folds without question until he gets to my red and black duffle containing my outfits for Subzero.

Before I can get to him from my position in the closet, tripping over hangers and empty bags, he holds up a mini camo leather skirt and brown leather bustier. "What is this little number?" He smirks, winking at me and whistling as he waves it around. "Haven't seen you wear this one yet," he jokes, pulling it out of my grasp when I try to take it from him.

I whip the bag off the bed so he can't pull anything else out and try to yank the camo one from his grip one more time, and he concedes. "Marco buys me these," I say under my breath, turning down the radio and throwing the bag into the closet. Marco has purchased all of my little outfits so far, wanting me to look good and feel comfortable as I wasn't one of the girls to walk around barely clothed like Melody and Shae. "I'm working on payin' him back," I defend when Jude gives me a raised eyebrow look.

"Yeah sure," his quirks, taking his right hand and making a loose fist, thrusting it up and down toward his mouth while making sucking and slurping sounds.

"Payin' him back." He smirks, winking, and I slap him hard in the chest, the sound echoing through the room. He flinches back, grabbing my wrist and pulling me down on his lap.

His fingers go to my chin and I can see his eyes running over my bruise as Marco's had earlier. I pull from his grasp, trying to playfully kick him off, but his demeanor is now serious. "Marco said to watch out for you," he mumbled, pointing to my cheek, "is that why?"

"Soon to be ex-husband," I say with a shrug, flicking my hand up toward my face and standing from the bed, returning to putting clothes away. "You don't have to worry 'bout me Jude." I turn back and wink, seeing him shake his head and return to folding.

"Alright then," he mutters with a snort, handing me a group of t-shirts. "Just know you can call me, okay?" he asks, giving me a side long look and I nod. He helps me late into the afternoon, exchanging phone numbers as the sun first starts to disappear and he jogs away toward his trailer, three up and two across.

Running a brush through my dark hair and throwing on a red knit hat, I pull on a pair of brown boots, grabbing my American flag purse from the coat rack and I'm out the door, stopping to touch up my cover-up job on my bruise in the side mirror before cranking my car to life. I honk as I pass Jude's trailer and am texting Rhea as I turn out onto the road, headed for her and Chad's house.

"You know I coulda used you like an hour ago," Rhea yells to me as soon as I walk in her front door, shaking off the chill of the setting sun. I mumble a reply, throwing my purse into one of the dining room chairs as I hear her coming down the stairs and I turn to her with a smile.

I am in awe of my cousin, slightly limping toward me with her four month old son on her hip. After being shot three times by her crazy stalker, Duke Orr, back in October, Rhea had under gone months of physical therapy, being limp free most days. Her hair is growing out, slow but sure, and her extensions that had been attached by her best friend, Kendall, are at her shoulders now, curled and looking perfect. Holding my arms out, she scoops Charlie off her hip and into them and I hug him to my chest, kissing his forehead a bunch of times as he gurgles and coos at me, grabbing at my shirt.

"I thought you were gonna text me when you got to your trailer?" she pointedly says, giving me a sharp look while she stacks solo cups to take outside. I can see from the corner of my eye that the fire is already roaring out there in the yard but I don't want to look any further, knowing Bobby is already out there as his truck is on the street. He'll make me lose all train of thought right now.

"I got side tracked." I sigh, bouncing Charlie lightly on my hip as he sucks on his hand. Rhea huffs, throwing her hand to her hip and rolling her eyes at me, and I grin. "A neighbor helped me unpack. A neighbor I happen to work with at Marco's club." She mumbled something that I didn't catch but cut off my question as she starts to dump ice into a glass pitcher. She knows I work for Marco, but she doesn't know I dance. Rhea, along with everyone else for that matter, thinks I do the books and tend bar at times at one of Marco's dive bars, also in Waverly. What they don't know won't hurt them, right?

"I'll dress the lil' guy up before we take him out there." I change the subject, seeing his little boots and coat on the table top, and I plop down in the chair, sitting him squarely on my lap. His chubby little legs oppose me putting the boots on his feet, but I give him some kisses and he squeals, forgetting what I'm doing as I hear the sliding glass door open.

"Well, hey Ellie," Chad's deep, smooth voice reaches me and I look up to see him standing near my shoulder, his blue eyes looking down on his son, moving over me and immediately frowning. His fingers go to my chin, bringing the right side of my face into his view as his eyes are burning a hole into my skin.

"What the hell? Rhea, did you see this?" he grinds out, motioning for my cousin to come to his side as I push his hand away, tugging on Charlie's jacket with my face down.

"Leave it alone," I say, handing the baby to him and standing, moving my way to the other side of the table to put some space between us. I can feel Rhea's eyes roaming me, and meeting them I can see her squint, trying to make out what her husband was freaking out about. I turn my cheek to her and motion at it. Obviously my make-up hadn't covered it as well as I had thought and her eyes go wide. My eye is still half red from the broken blood vessel. She quickly makes her way in front of me, touching my skin lightly with her fingertips.

"What do you mean leave it alone, Ell? When did he do this?" The concern in her voice breaks through my stubborn layer and I look her in the eye, seeing the sadness in the blue-grey depths. I don't want anyone to worry about me, so I rub my hand up her arm, patting her on the shoulder and giving her a lopsided grin.

"He surprised me last night at the old trailer, but he left before I could call anyone," I lie, trying to get them to back off. But I can see Chad standing near the door, his eyes like steel on us. This is the SEAL that will forever be in him. The protector. He wants to defend me, but I can't let him risk his government job with NCIS just to get a little revenge.

"Please?" I turn my attention back to Rhea, pulling her in a hug that at first she tries to fight, but eventually gives in, hugging me back. "I'm okay. It's just a bruise."

"Just a bruise," Chad scoffs, giving me an angry look. "Next time it'll just be a broken arm or leg. Hell, Ellie, what if he decides not to leave one night and you can't get to a phone?" His voice is raising and it'll undoubtedly draw others into the house so I move over closer to him, locking my eyes on his.

"And if I moved in here, it would just bring him here. What if you weren't home one day? He would threaten Rhea and Charlie. I'd rather die than let that happen," I grind out, my fists clenching at my sides. I'd let Jake kill me if it meant he'd never threaten what family I have left.

"At least we'd know you'd be safe here, with people nearby that you can go to for help if you need it," Rhea says softly, placing both hands on my shoulders from behind, pulling me into a side hug and resting her head on my shoulder. "Dana is nearby, along with Rosa and Reno. Kendall's family is down the road," she continues to list off the people I could go to, and I put my hand up to stop her.

"I'm okay guys," I plead, taking Charlie from his

father and hugging him between his mother and I. "Now come on, let's go have some fun with these guys before they ship off." They both nod, Chad helping Rhea with a sweatshirt and carrying a pitcher of tea for her as we head out in to the chilled, fading sun.

There he is and he takes my breath away almost automatically. His tall lean figure is framed perfectly in jeans and a tight t-shirt with a flannel over top and a hooded sweatshirt, unzipped to seemingly showcase his torso just for me. His short dirty blonde hair is under a brimmed knit hat, cocked to the side, and he's propped up against the back of Chad's Silverado with the tail gate down. His hazel eyes spot me and a perfect smile caresses his freckle dotted face, making my heart stop.

I waggle my fingers at him and immediately kick myself silently, smiling back at him as I head over to Rhea to hand over her son. I feel so stupid. I feel like a school girl again. It scares the shit out of me.

~~~~

# BOBBY

"Bobby's catchin' flies again guys, watch out!" I hear Fred Black joke as he elbows my arm, but I don't avert my eyes from that pretty little thing walking on the other side of the bonfire following Rhea. Her blue-green eyes dart my way again and I give her another sideways smirk, tipping my beer at her; which I can tell makes her giggle as she leans into Rhea and whispers something to her.

"You're just jealous, ol' man," I finally retort, knocking my SEAL team mate in the back and making him spill his glass of beer on the front of his jeans. He grumbles over his shoulder at me as he wipes at the foam and I just laugh, taking another sip from my Bud Light and looking back to Ellie, finding Rhea staring at me. Her look tells me there's something wrong, but as I look at her she nods to Ellie and shakes her head slowly, quietly telling me to stay back like she has since I first met her cousin.

"Don't worry, brother," my LT, Austin French, says, throwing his arm around my shoulder while taking a long chug from a bottle of Jack Daniels then handing it to me, "I'll go do some recon and see what's good." He grins and winks, patting me hard on the shoulder as he adjusts his Navy baseball cap, leaving my side and heading straight for Ellie. I wasn't going to worry about him; he does this every time Ellie is involved. He'll go over there, flirt shamelessly with her making her giggle and laugh, riling her up to the point where she has to come over to our little group to dispel the lies he'll feed to her. It's all in his 'wingman' repertoire, which he uses well.

"Aren't ya worried that LT will steal your girl, Timmons?" I turn to see one of our new members, Lenny Hale, leaning on Chad's tailgate next to me; his long neck craned as he's watching French approach Ellie. I snort and shrug my shoulders, taking another drag from my beer bottle, followed by a swift chug of the Jack. Lenny is short and stocky, his forehead only coming up to about my shoulder, but he's tough as nails.

"Nah, I'm not worried, Len," I mumble and he nods in reply, flicking his eyes from mine to LT, then behind us to our other SEAL Team members. Am I worried? Jealous, maybe, but worried? No way.

Slipping my eyes over the others gathered around closer to the fire, I stop on Ellie again. Her littlest mannerisms seem to pull at something inside me I've never felt before. The way she brushes her short hair back behind her ear, only to have to do it again seconds later. The slight smile that quirks up on one corner of her mouth as French probably tells her some exaggerated hero story, then the giggle that follows makes me want to run over and throw my arms around her, pulling her close to feel her laugh glide over my skin. I've never felt this way about anyone, let alone some girl I've only carried on small conversations with. There's just something about her that makes my heart jump up and beat to a different tune.

There's something about her that makes me wish I still had a family to take her home to. My adoptive parents would have loved Ellie and her quirky little smile. They would have loved how her laugh seems to fill everyone with happiness.

My real parents, Ellis and Mary Jetts, died in a car accident when I was five years old, leaving me with no immediate family, so I was put into the State of Georgia's foster care. I bounced around from hell hole to hell hole, getting smacked around by drunken foster fathers who only took in kids for the state money; until I was ten years old.

My tenth birthday brought salvation; at least I see it that way. My social worker, the sweet Darla Knight, had taken me from a dirty trailer filled with other filthy children, to a big, open dairy farm in rural Georgia. That day I met hard-headed Harlis Timmons and his wife, Betty, and I immediately knew I wanted to live there. They adopted me two weeks later, and I owe who I am today to their great parenting. Harlis had been older, ten years Betty's senior, and a Navy veteran, pushing me to always do my best in everything. He taught me the value of hard work on that dairy farm and working weekends with his brother in their co-owned construction business. Betty was sweet and caring when it came to helping me win girls over, and she also taught me how to bake a mean apple pie.

Even now thinking about the day they died makes me mad and I take a long swig of beer to stop from grinding my teeth too hard. It was two months before my high school graduation and the Georgia State Troopers showed up at my little school, pulling me into the main office to deliver the news. Two twenty-something drug addicts had cornered my mom and dad in the kitchen not long after I had left for school, supposedly demanding money. The cops had deduced, and it no doubt happened, that Harlis had gone for the shotgun he always kept in the hallway closet and the two guys had shot him and Betty to death, taking the two hundred dollars that was in the coffee can on the fridge.

I had been torn up for weeks, not really attending school except for test days because I was eighteen and they couldn't force me to go. I signed the papers to turn over the dairy farm to my uncle, Harlis' brother, and on the day of graduation, with my cap and gown still on, I walked into the closest Navy recruiter's office, signing up for the next basic training ship-out date. I haven't been back to that little farming town since. It would be too hard for me to see who I once was, compared to the man I am now.

I know deep down that good ol' Harlis and Betty would be proud of me if they were still alive. They'd see what I see when I come off a mission. I'm helping the weak. I'm saving those in need and righting what wrongs I can. I'm doing what my country needs me to do and I'm being a good sailor, just like in the stories Harlis use to tell me of his Navy days.

Fingers wrapping around my bicep bring me from my day dreaming and I move my eyes from the fire down to those pretty little blue-green pools staring up at me. *God, she even smells good,* I quickly think to myself and smile down at her, loving the tiny giggle that escapes her perfect lips.

"What can I do for you, Miss Ellie?" I ask, squaring my body to stand right in front of her as she keeps giggling, looking over her shoulder and pointing.

"Is that man always full of it, or just when he's around me?" She laughs and I can't help but smile, fighting off the urge to brush her hair behind her ear and let my touch linger on her cheek. I follow her gaze, taking in the scene she is laughing at.

French is up on top of one of the picnic tables, his shirt off in the cold February air, and he's animatedly telling some sort of story with pretty much everyone's eyes on him. Taking a swig from the bottle of whiskey I am holding onto, I reach around Ellie, offering it to her while discreetly brushing my arm along her

33

middle pulling her a little closer to me. She takes it from me, and with a sweet little grin wraps her lips around it, tipping it back while I tamp down the need to be that bottle. To be the thing with her lips pressed up against it. Damn, I'm not use to feeling like this.

Shaking my head, I turn my attention back to my LT and shout, "Put your shirt back on, ol' man." He turns toward me and flips me off, flexing at the same time as he's trying to show off.

"You're just jealous, boy." He laughs along with everyone else, but jumps down, accepting a helping hand from Chad and Reno as he wobbles, trying to put his shirt back on. The man sure does like to celebrate and as they leave him alone in one of the lawn chairs I can hear him grumble that he was just having a good time. I laugh at him quietly, Ellie turning on me with the whiskey still in her hand.

"And what is so funny, mister?" she quips, her hand on her hip as she gives me a killer sexy look, taking another sip from the bottle. If she only knew what she was doing to me. I shrug my shoulders and lean back against Chad's truck, smiling as she rolls her eyes at me. My shoulders tense and I shoot my hand out, taking her chin as gentle as I can between my thumb and fingers, turning her right side to me as I lower my face to within a whisper of hers.

"What the hell, Ellie?" I grind out, trying to keep it in a whisper to not draw attention from my SEAL Team buddies nearby. Her eye is red, framing the beautiful blue-green and taking out the white. She tries to brush my grip from her skin, but I don't let go. "Tell me," I try to say with a little softness, trying not to let this anger seep out at her.

"Stop," she says, yanking my fingers from her chin

and looking down at the ground, shaking her head. "Don't be like Chad and Rhea." She sighs, finally looking up at me. I can see the tears lingering on her lashes.

"Chief and I are cut from the same cloth," I defend my acting overprotective like Chad. Stepping even closer to her so that she has to crane her neck back, I wrap my arm around her shoulders and pull her in, almost losing all control of the situation as I feel her arms wrap around my waist. "Why don't you take Rhea's invitation and move in here?" I whisper into her hair, feeling her stiffen a tiny bit. "You know I'd feel a lot better if you did."

"No," she laughs cynically, "you'd know I was under lock and key, with watchful eyes on me twenty-four-seven." She is right. I just wish I could force that asshole of a husband to sign the divorce papers and get this whole situation over for her. There are a couple of ways I could make him sign them, using my many acquired skills, but that would probably just make more problems. I squeeze my arm around her shoulders a little more and feel her relax, her arms tightening around my waist as she snuggles her cheek into my chest.

"Just promise me you'll call Chad if he comes around while I'm gone," I ask and she scoffs. I don't understand why she lets that bastard get away with this shit. He needs to be in jail and deserves to be dead according to the stories I've heard about her past from Chad, filtered through Rhea. She's afraid, I know, but there comes a point where she shouldn't be afraid anymore. She needs to feel safe and loved. A piece of me hopes she'll let me try and be the person who lets her feel that way.

Shifting, she rests her chin on my chest and I can't help but scrutinize her eye, moving my gaze to the make-up covered flesh surrounding it and noticing the bruise underneath. As I run my thumb over it softly, her eyes flutter shut for a split second, making my heart ache while a smile caresses her lips.

"Okay," she whispers, opening her eyes slowly.

I swear, her eyes could burn a path straight to my heart. As she looks up at me, I keep my hand on her soft face, running my thumb along her cheek. She leans the slightest bit into my touch and I squeeze her tighter to my chest. I feel her rising up on the tips of her toes, her eyes zooming in on my lips and I feel myself leaning down slightly when a loud throat clearing comes from the bonfire.

"Hey Ellie," Garth's voice rings out over the stereo, and she snaps her head away from me. Kicking myself mentally, I flick my eyes over to where the guy is standing with his boyfriend, Brad, by the fire with beers in hand waving at this sweet little thing in my arms. Talk about a cock-block. Garth always seems to cut in on Ellie and me when we were talking or flirting. Makes me wonder sometimes.

"I gotta go see what they want." She sighs, waving back and looking up at me, a slight blush running over her cheeks. I grin at her and the red deepens as she releases my waist, holding the bottle of Jack up, and then taking a long swig and handing it to me after wiping her mouth with the back of her hand. Reaching out, I cover her hand with mine, running my thumb over the back of it and trying to convey that I want her to stay here, with me. Her eyes flick from mine to our hands and a small, sexy smile caresses her lips. She's such a minx and she doesn't even realize it.

"Come on back," I say softly, trying to lace it with as much of my charm as I can because I don't want this stolen moment to be over. She giggles, quickly nodding then heading off toward the fire. She glances back over her shoulder and I nod at her, drinking the last of my beer and tossing the bottle into the metal barrel, never taking my eyes from her.

"Damn; if I didn't know better, Timmons, I'd be thinkin' you got it hard for that girl," Black's familiar tease comes over my shoulder and I lean against the tailgate of Chad's truck, making sure I can still see that pretty little thing as she laughs and jokes with the two men. "Yup," I hear him laugh and I turn on him, throwing a slow punch that he easily blocks.

"You'll keep your thoughts to yourself if ya know what's good for ya," I teasingly threaten, throwing another light punch and connecting with his ribs. I laugh as he backs away, shaking his head at me as our other team members join in on the laugh, throwing insults and ribs out into the fire lit night air. They are right, though. I think I have it bad for this girl and I have no idea how to deal.

I join the guys, telling stories and drinking beers and all the while keeping my eye on Ellie across the yard for the rest of the night. I'm not going to lie, I get a little jealous when she sits on Garth and then Brad's laps, their hands on her waist, so close to her perfect behind, but I shake it off each time. I have no right to be jealous. Hell, we haven't even really talked all that much let alone gone on a date. Sure we've flirted, but it's been fleeting like the moment earlier. Nothing more than simple touches shared, followed by a blush flowing over her pretty face.

Friends start to leave; Black and Austin pass out in their trucks, along with the other guys passing out on the living room floor as Chad and I make our way into his house, careful to step over the snoring Uclid. I just laugh at my spotter, kicking him lightly and hearing him grumble then just roll over, too drunk to really care.

"Do you need anythin', man?" Chief asks, slapping a hand on my shoulder lightly. I shake my head and look him in the face, seeing his eyes skirt up the stairs and wink at me. Marriage and a baby still haven't changed this man before me. I laugh at him, shoving open the door to the downstairs bedroom that he and Rhea are letting me occupy for the night.

"Alright then, Bobby." He smiles, patting me on the back. "Oh and by the way," he stops and turns back to me from the bottom of the stairs, "Ellie is upstairs, but if you have any sympathy in your body at all for the lecture I would have to endure if something did happen, *please,* stay down here." I fake salute him, and he flips me off as he quietly jogs up the stairs.

Stripping down to my boxers while trying not to fall over, I shuffle my way past my passed out friends into the bathroom off the kitchen, squinting when I flick on the light. *Why the hell do they have to be so bright?* Splashing my face with hot water and brushing my teeth, I laugh at my reflection in the mirror. I even look drunk, my hair sticking up from the hat I had on earlier and my eyes slightly blood shot. Kicking Uclid one more time when I pass back through and laughing when he tries unsuccessfully to grab my ankle, I stumble my way into the dark bedroom, leaving the door cracked and tumbling in under the sheets.

I just lay there, not able to get Ellie out of my head. Her smile and the way it seems to seep into my heart even when she isn't around makes me laugh to myself and I throw my arm over my eyes, trying to force myself to sleep. Chad's house is quiet except for the snoring drunks out in the living room and I just lay there, trying to not let the numerous fantasies run through my head. I need the sleep. We ship out tomorrow night to some God forsaken jungle.

"Bobby?" the sweet little voice breaks through the silence. Jerking my arm from my eyes I lean my face up to see Ellie, her pretty little face shadowed in the dark as she's peeking around the door. I just kind of grunt a reply and she pushes the door open. "Can I join you?" she quietly whispers as I sit up on my elbows, her tiny figure framed by the weak light coming from Chad and Rhea's kitchen. She slowly, hesitantly walks toward me, her hands clasped tightly in front of her as she worries her bottom lip, looking so innocently sexy that I have to rub my eyes to make sure I'm not dreaming.

"Bobby?" she whispers again, kicking my brain back into reality mode even though there's a rampant fantasy playing in my groin. She's at the edge of the bed now, her beautiful blue-green eyes bearing down on me. "I just want to cuddle." She bites her lip again and I have to fight off everything in my nature not to pull her sweet little face to mine and kiss her crazy. Then, of course, it leading to other things.

"Wha....well yeah," I stumble on the words while fumbling with the comforter, lifting it up so she can slide in. *Is this really happening?* I think to myself. *Is this little angel really climbing in to cuddle with me?* Her little legs and hips shimmy in next to me and she lays her head in the crux of my shoulder as I wrap my arm around her shoulders. It feels right. It feels different than anything I've had before and I like it.

"When you get back, we'll have to put all this shit behind us and you can take me to dinner because you make me feel good," she mumbles, and I can feel her smile against my shoulder. It feels good knowing she's happy in my arms, and I let a little laugh out as I run my fingers through her short, dark hair.

"Of course, Sweetheart. We'll go wherever you want." Hell, as of right now I'd walk through the desert and back to take this girl to dinner, that's how I'm feeling right now. It scares the shit out of me how she seems to get under my skin, but it's thrilling at the same time. I want this. I want her, and I want her to want me.

She gives a content little sigh, her warm breath washing over my shirt and bringing my nerves to life. It seems like her perfumed scent is wrapping around my heart and I turn my face into her hair, tucking her a little closer. "Goodnight Bobby," she sweetly mutters, shattering part of my heart with her simple need of wanting me to cuddle.

"Goodnight Sweetheart, and happy birthday," I whisper softly, kissing the crown of her head and letting my touch linger, smiling when she squirms closer into my side. Her bare legs wrap around mine, her skin burning into mine, and I wonder if she feels it too. I'm betting she does, because the second the thought crosses my mind, her arm over my chest tightens just the slightest bit and I kiss her hair again.

This is a perfect send off, even if we do still have our clothes on. Sleeping in the arms of someone who needs me. In the arms of someone I seem to be needing. Someone that I want, no matter how long I have to wait.

# CHAPTER 3

*Ellie*

*March 2, 2013*

"You're late, girly," I hear Melody's sarcastic little chime echo through the tiny hall as I shove my way into the bustling back entrance of Subzero Strip Club, my only current employer. Fellow dancers tell me 'hello' as I smile and pass them, squeezing my way between Big Joe, the tipping three hundred pounds security guard who is permanently plastered to the dressing room door, and his current eye candy, the voluptuous Miss Gina.

Melody gives me a fake angry look from her reflection in the wall length mirror as I throw my small bag down into my normal chair on her left. Her hair is down and curled, being multi colored with light pink, blue, and purple. Her light mocha skin looks wonderful with the pastels and I playfully kiss her on the cheek as she painstakingly tries to apply eyeliner, swatting at me as I laugh and plop down into my chair. "You know you're up in like ten minutes right, Ell?"

"Yeah, yeah." I sigh, reaching into my bag and pulling out the outfit I had planned for tonight. There Is no shame in the back room of a strip club and I had learned real quick that no one is really looking; so shimmying out of the jeans, tank and shirt, I begin pulling on the skimpy leather skirt and red bandeau top. Checking my reflection in the mirror, I adjust the top a little and zip up the side zipper of the skirt. Pulling the knee high stiletto boots from the cubby Melody and I share, I sigh and tug them on, wincing at the tight feel on my toes. "I'll never get used to these," I grumble, leaning forward to start applying my makeup.

A couple of the girls giggle around me and Melody huffs, spinning her chair to face me. The pastel glitter eye shadow curls up from her eyelids, making her look like a magical creature with the pixie costume she has on. Tonight is the monthly 'fantasy' night here at Subzero, almost all of the girls dressing up as some sort of sexy magical creature. Me, well I am going to be a sexy devil, pinning my hair back fast and pulling on the bright red wig from the counter. I really hate myself deep down for doing this job, but I need to pay my bills and Jake had ruined every other possible job opportunity for me with threats to local business owners over the last few months.

"Have you heard from that cutie; what's his name… Bobby?" Mel asks me, tapping her manicured nails on the counter beside my elbow as I lean into the mirror, applying mascara and eyeliner like she had done only minutes before. Red and black are my main colors tonight and as I sweep the red glitter filled liquid shadow over my lid, I release a big sigh. I haven't heard from him in two weeks and it makes me anxious.

"Nah, but Rhea says that at times she didn't hear from Chad for an entire month." It makes me feel a bit better when Rhea reminds me that she's been through this, but with me it's different. Bobby and I aren't even dating; hell, we haven't even kissed! The waiting is the hard part and at times I wonder if slipping into his bed and cuddling with him the night of the party was a mistake. He had slipped out silently early that morning, leaving me with a sweet little note that even now is tucked into my purse, snuggled between my debit card and driver's license. I can't help but think about him a lot; his sexy ass smile and lean, defined body. It makes a slight shiver roll over my skin and goose-bumps appear immediately.

Melody's hand on my shoulder snaps me out of my daydream and I focus back on her reflection in the mirror. "You're up in two." She smiles, kissing my cheek. "Go get it, girl."

She giggles and leaves me to go mingle with the

other girls, eventually making her way out into the bar like we all do to try and make some tips delivering drinks and so on and so forth. I may not like this job, but the money is good most of the time and the power trip I get is almost high like. Those men out there, they'd do anything I tell them to do for a dance most nights. I laugh to myself and put my little horns over my wig, grabbing the prop whip from my bag and heading out into the hall.

"Knock'em dead, Ell." Big Joe winks, his massive build leaned back against the red velvet covered wall in his barstool, Miss Gina on his lap. I wiggle my fingers at him and try to avert my eyes from Gina's hand down the front of his jeans, but I can't help the tiny blush that runs over my skin, and Joe laughs, disappearing as I round the corner to the stage stairs.

The stairs are clear, lighted from within with glitter covering the outside, making rays of different color light bounce off the black leather of my shoes as I make my way up. The last few verses of Def Leppard's 'Pour Some Sugar On Me' pounds out from the sound system as my heart picks up its rhythm, just like every time I take the stage. I can't help it. I get nervous.

With my fingers gripping the black curtains, I peek around them to see the crowd. A little fear spikes up in my heart, wondering if there will be someone in the crowd who will recognize me, but I tamp it down and try to calm my heart beat. The pulsing red and blue lights from Harlem's performance are still dancing around as she finishes her routine, picking the money from the stage as she shakes it for a few more guys, shoving more money into her thong. She swipes a handful of bills and pulls a customer to the edge of the stage, giving him an up close and personal feel of her DD size boob job, then smiles and shoves him back into his seat, grinning the entire time she saunters back toward me.

"You're turn, little girl." She giggles, swatting me on the butt as she pulls on a silk robe hung strategically behind the curtain. I give her a halfhearted smirk and try to take a deep breath again, my hands shaking like they usually do when it comes my time to take this scarlet stage.

The DJ turns the red and blue lights of Harlem's show into red and white for me, playing orange and yellow all across the expansive room to look like flames. "Alright gentlemen, you better hold on to your seats," the deep voice of Marco comes over the club and I can't help but smile. "Now coming to the stage is the seductress of demons, the bringer of darkness, and the catcher of sinners' souls. Please welcome, Vixen!" Whistles, shouts, and the sounds of clapping hands drown out the first couple beats of my song, but I know I have four sets of a four count to walk out before the lyrics of Halestorm's "I Get Off" kick in.

*"You don't know that I know, You watch me every night,"* and that power trip hits me. I can feel the eyes on me. It's like that inkling feeling you get when you think you're being followed, but this is from an entire room full of men. *"Your greedy eyes upon me, And then I come undone, I could close the curtain, But this is too much fun."* The chorus kicks in and I wrap my hands around the pole, pulling myself up and keeping my legs to the side, flipping myself upside down with learned ease and wrapping my knees around the cold metal.

I've learned it's better not to look at the crowd

unless you're working them on the edge of the stage, so keeping my mind on the spin, I slowly descend the pole until my shoulders hit the stage, rolling into a split and giving the group of men at the closest table a great view of my red lace thong. They cheer and toss their money near me and I just go on with the song, working the stage and hitting the moves that Melody had worked out for me to the best of my ability.

The music and my setting eventually fade in my head and I'm back in West Virginia, in a ballet studio working on my pointe. Keeping my leg straight as I spin and pointing my toes perfectly with every chance. Sharp clean movements until the cheering of the crowd breaks through my dream and I'm slowly crawling on my hands and knees toward a patron at the edge of the stage, the final few beats of my routine thrumming through the speakers as I take the money he holds out in my teeth, seeing the twenty something man rake his eyes over every inch of me.

"A big hand for Vixen," Marco's deep voice announces and the cheers and yells ring out as I stand, wagging my fingers at the men as they toss more money out onto the stage. One man I know as a regular waves me over to his spot on the right side of the stage and as I bend over, accepting a kiss on the cheek as he tucks some bills into the waist of my skirt, my eyes spot what I think is a familiar face toward the back of the club.

Squinting, I think I see Jake's partner, Tom Walden, posted up at the edge of the bar, his tall, dark haired frame sipping a drink with his eyes locked on me. Fear rises in my heart, making my chest feel tight and as I slowly make my way back to the curtain I try to keep my eye on him. I'm praying furiously that it's not him, but the more I look, the more he keeps eye contact and I'm certain it's him. Panic takes over and I dart around the black curtain, almost tripping in my heels down the glitter stairs.

I'm hoping he didn't recognize me. I have the wig and makeup on and he was sort of far away, but why is he here in the first place? Coming around the corner into the hallway, I keep my eyes on the floor, but can still see Gina on her knees in front of Big Joe, his hands in her hair and his pants around his ankles. I put my hand up to shield the view, slipping into the dressing room amongst the bodyguards grunts in approval of her actions.

"Well, hold on a second, she's right here," my face pops up to see Melody with my cell phone up to her ear. My breathing is erratic as fear still fills my veins, shaking my limbs and I see a confused look pass over her features. Putting her hand over the phone she whispers, "What's wrong?" moving my bag so I can plop down into my stool.

"I thought I saw someone," I dismiss her, trying to calm my breathing as I reach for my cell still in her hand. I point and mouth the word "who" and she smiles wide, handing me the phone and animatedly plopping down in her stool next to me. With her chin in her hand, she leans toward me with a sly smile. I'm almost afraid to see who is on the phone with her animated state, but I put it to my ear.

"Hello?" I say, trying to keep the shakiness in and resting my arms on the counter in front of me.

"Well hello, Sweetheart," the smooth voice flows out, into my heart and I have to close my eyes. He doesn't know what the mere thought of him does to me. My anxiety and fear are gone instantly and my

49

heart starts racing for another reason. A wonderful reason.

~~~~~

# BOBBY

*Afghanistan*

"If you're not gonna listen, the LT is gonna have your head. Jackass," Uclid huffs as he pushes up off the ground beside me, leaving his spotter position in our shooting practice. I take my gaze from the scope of my rifle to see him shed his flak and toss it onto the front of the Hummer to my right. "You gotta get your head straight, Timmons, before he kicks both our asses."

"Yeah, yeah," I shake him off and return my attention back to the long range target down wind, zooming in on it with a few clicks of my scope. There's little wind and I take my time, adjusting for it and finally squeezing the trigger. Seeing my target explode in a cloud of dust as the .300 Winchester Mag finds its mark, I grin to myself. God I love my job. Letting the dust settle, I make sure my gun is safe to transport and snap down the legs, slinging the strap over my shoulder while hopping to my feet.

Uclid is right, though. I have been off my game for the last week or so since we've been here at the base in the mountains. I'm not going to lie, my thoughts have been elsewhere. With a cute little thing sitting on the tailgate of my jacked up Chevy with her bare legs swinging in the light breeze. The smell of her as she lay in my arms that night at Chad's house and the way her breathing sounded like music to my ears; playing a tune only my heart could understand. Yeah that might sound soft, but it's the truth and right now I need to face the truth. I've got it hard for Ellie.

That night, tangled in her arms with her skin against mine, I fell hard. Ever since I had to pry myself from her, leaving her with a kiss on the forehead and a note, I can't get her out of my head and heart. It's been killing me and I'm not used to feeling like this. I've never let a woman get to me this bad, but I kind of like it.

That first couple of days away from her were the worst. In the hot, sticky jungle of South America, I could smell her at every turn. Sloshing through mud and muck, I thought I heard Ellie call my name, but it was all in my head and heart. I had to snap out of it and 'cowboy-up' as we call it. Get my game face on and be the SEAL I need to be.

We had trudged through the jungle, meeting our objective and demolishing a drug cartel's hideout, rescuing some U.S. embassy captives in their hold and have been in the hot mountains of Afghanistan ever since. I hate this fucking place. It's a hell hole. There is nothing but people who despise us, heat during the day and freezing temps at night. I can't wait until I'm on U.S. soil again. I can't wait until I can take that sweet little thing on a date.

"Timmons," I snap from my musing to wheel on Uclid, seeing him far ahead of me and making his way back to the barracks, "get your fuckin' head outta the clouds and hustle up," he yells over his shoulder while shaking his head and I jog after him, my longer legs catching his in seconds as my rifle swings along on my shoulder. My spotter and buddy is mumbling to himself as we get to the barracks, tossing our gear off and sitting to clean our weapons.

Silence surrounds us; the only sounds being that of mumbled speech coming from the bunks and the random clicks and slides of the parts of our weapons. I can't be quiet anymore. He's my best friend. "There's just somethin' about her," I say, putting the last pieces of equipment away and standing to stretch and strip of the sweaty material and seeing some sand drop out.

"I know." He laughs, giving me an evil grin. Disappearing around into the barracks I cringe when I hear him yell, "Timmons admitted it, guys. He's got it hard for Miss Ellie." The laughs that fill the room make me not want to go in there because I can just imagine the shit they are going to say.

Me. The playboy. The womanizer. I've finally been struck by the bug. Putting on a tough face I round the corner to see them all gathered around on the couches and chairs. Vipers in a pit, that's what they are. Wolves surrounding a wounded buffalo, waiting and biding their time with sly grins on their faces.

They all join in on a group "Ohhh", pointing and laughing, while Black just sits back and smiles, shaking his head at me as I sit down next to him. "Tol' ya, boy," he says, hitting me in the shoulder while handing me a water bottle.

"You tol' me what, ol' man," I quip, still fending off other comments from the other guys as Lenny starts to lightly strum away on his Gibson. They throw out *'You'll never stay tied down'* and *'You haven't even had it and you're pussy whipped already'*, making me chuckle and shake my head as Black slaps his hand on my shoulder.

"I tol' ya that that girl was special." He smiles, sparing a look over to French sitting on his other side, who nods, grinning almost unbearably as the guys still joke around me. Fred Black had told me that Ellie was special, on New Year's when we were at Chad and Rhea's house for a little get together. I had brushed him off, thinking then that I was just planning on hooking up with Ellie, but now it's different. Now she strikes a different chord, just like Lenny on his guitar as he changes tempo.

They kept making fun of me into the afternoon, through dinner, and even back in the barracks. When the time came that we had a second to use the computers, the guys flocked to them like moths to a flame, all wanting to call their families and girls back home, but I just flopped down on my bunk with a satellite phone in hand.

I have Ellie's number memorized from all the text messages we sent back and forth since meeting. Staring at the rails of the bunk above me, I smile at the picture taped up there. It was from Chad and Rhea's wedding, when we were all out on the patio during the reception. Chad and Rhea were front and center, their love evident even through the lens of the camera while Ellie and I sat to Chad's right, my arm around her shoulders that were covered by my coat. She is so beautiful it almost hurts to look at her smiling face. It's even harder on my heart to remember that she was leaning ever so slightly toward me as the photographer was snapping the pictures, eventually leaning her head on my shoulder as I snuggled her into my side and trying to ward off the chilly January air. How much time have I wasted with her?

Punching in the numbers, I wait while it dials. I try not to let the nerves bother me as I wait to hear her voice, the *need* to hear it thrumming through my veins like crazy. After four rings I'm thinking I should hang up when an unfamiliar female voice says hello. "Ellie?" I question.

"No, this is Melody. Who's this?" the perky woman replies and I let out a silent sigh, recognizing the name of Ellie's friend from one of our past conversations. After telling her who I am, I cringe at the squeal that rings out, taking the phone from my ear and shaking my head to try and stop the ringing. "Oh, well she's out at the bar."

"Oh," I try not to sound too disappointed, even though I am. "Just tell her I called and that I'm thinkin' 'bout her, okay?" Did that sound too stupid? I hope it doesn't because I can't take it back now.

"Okay," she says and I'm about to say my thanks when she cuts in. "Well, hold on a second, she's right here." My mood picks up a little and I can tell she covers the phone with something, the muffled voices and scratching sound coming through clear on my end.

I hear Melody ask what is wrong and Ellie reply something, then her sweet voice is loud and clear on the line. "Hello?" My heart jumps up at a mile a minute, threatening to beat right out of my skin. She does sound a bit flustered, but I push it off for now.

"Well hello, Sweetheart." I smile, knowing she'll

recognize that it's me right away. I love calling her sweetheart and I know it makes her feel good. I can hear her let out a contented sigh, and it breaks my heart. Does she miss me?

"Bobby, it's so good to hear your voice," she breathes out and the smile that finds my face almost reaches my ears. I wish I could see her face. I would give anything to see her pretty smile and those beautiful eyes looking back at me. "How are you, Bobby?"

"I'm as good as I can be." I laugh, scratching my hand back through my hair and feeling some sand fall out. I hate sand. "How about you, darlin'? Everything okay with you?" I just want to hear her voice. She could be telling me the most un-interesting story, but I'd listen all the same as long as she is telling it.

"I'm good, Bobby." She giggles and I can hear voices in the background as she tells someone to 'shush'. "Yeah it's been kinda cold here the last couple of days, but they say it will be nice soon. Rhea and I wanna take Charlie to the zoo with Rosa and Marisol." She tells me how Charlie is jabbering away more and more every day, sitting up and starting to crawl. She loves her little 'nephew' to death; it's evident in the pride in her voice.

"What about you, Ellie?" I laugh, smiling at the giddiness in her voice when she talks about her cousin and family. She cares about them and they are pretty much all she has, I know that, but I want to hear about her. I want to know how she's getting along with work and her new trailer. "Tell me about you," I say, trying not to fill it with all the desire I feel all of a sudden but I know on the other end, Ellie is probably flushing just the tiniest bit.

"I'm doin' good, Bobby." She giggles. "Work is good. The trailer is good. Same ol', same ol'. You know." I can hear the voices in the background again and she covers the phone, trying to muffle the sound of her telling them to 'fuck off' and I laugh loudly, getting some looks from the men around the room.

"But you, you're doing okay? No problems?" I say, meaning that Jake hasn't come around. I can hear her take a deep, annoyed breath and release it. She is getting sick of Chad and I bothering her about keeping herself safe. She should just move in with Rhea and Chad, but she's stubborn and independent, like her cousin.

"Yeah, no problems," she mumbles but it seems halfhearted. Like she's keeping something back but I'm not going to push it. "I'm at work right now and I thought I mighta saw Jake's partner, Tom, but I think it was just the lighting." A nervous laugh meets my ears, but it doesn't make the thought of her being stalked lighten in my mind.

I should tell her to have Marco check into it and then call Marco myself when I hang up with her, but no, I'll just leave it alone. I don't want to annoy her even before getting the chance to really get to know her. Don't want to overstep my bounds, now do I?

"Alright then, Sweetheart," I lay it on thick, grinning as she giggles, "I'll let you go. I don't know when the next time is I'll be able to call, but I'll try my best." It is the truth. Most nights we get back and are too tired to do anything but sleep, let alone carry on a conversation.

"Alright, Bobby, it was nice to hear from you," she says and I know if she was standing before me she'd have that sexy as hell smile on her red lips. Her blue-green eyes would seem to darken as the sun sets, the dark blue a deep contrast to the bright turquoise they turned in the sunlight. I'd have to take her face in my hands and kiss her crazy if I saw that right now, there is no doubt.

"You take care of yourself, Sweetheart." I don't want to say goodbye so I hang on. "Oh, did you like the note I left you?"

"I liked it very much, Bobby." She laughs and it makes my heart go crazy. "I'll talk to you later, Bobby."

"Sure will, Sweetheart." I almost cheer. She liked my note. She giggles another goodbye and then the line goes dead, nothing but the dial tone meeting my ears.

Laying the phone on my chest I just stare up at that picture and her smiling face. The note I had left her was short and simple, if not stupid, and I laugh to myself while recalling it.

"Ellie,

I'm so glad you slept by my side last night. I didn't want to wake you because you look so beautiful right now so I'm leaving you this to find you when you get up. I'm looking forward to coming home and taking you out on a date, one with just us and not everyone else around, like French LOL. Just know that last night was fun because of you and that I'll call you when I get the chance. Take care of yourself and let Chad help you when you need it. You're beautiful, Sweetheart.

--Bobby"

It was simple. Yes. Sappy, hell yes, but she was looking like an angel that morning with her dark, short hair spread out on the pillow. I had wanted to stay so bad, but I have a duty. I am a sailor, a SEAL, and I love it. I wouldn't trade it for anything.

I will take her on a date when we get back home, and it will be the best date she's ever been on. Maybe even the best date I've ever been on, and I'm okay with that. Leaning back, I see that Uclid is leaning over the edge of his bunk above me, batting his eyes and making obnoxious kissing noises. Swiftly kicking the bottom of his bunk, I laugh as he cries out in pain, hopping down and holding his ass where my boot connected with it.

"Serves you right, asshole," I yell at him and settle back down. Well, he deserved it for breaking my sweet little day dream.

# I Never Asked You To Save Me

# CHAPTER 4

## BOBBY

*March 31, 2013*

*Afghanistan*

"Remind me why we volunteered to do this

again?" Uclid asks from his position at the opposite door of the Hummer we are riding in, going on patrol with a group of Grunts. I just mumble, shaking my head with a smile and adjusting my sunglasses to try and shade out that damn desert sun. It's got to be over one hundred degrees right now, but being here is better than just sitting in my bunk and thinking about Ellie.

No matter how much running, how much training we did, my thoughts still go back to her. Her beautiful face, those stunning eyes, her kissable lips; I'm lost within a daydream every second I can get if I'm not occupied, so that's why I pushed Uclid to take the empty spots on this patrol with me.

Two of the Marines who are in this platoon are in the infirmary currently, suffering from a heavy case of food poisoning, and I needed to have some time to not be lost in her. Not that I don't like thinking about that sweet little thing, but I have a job.

Our little caravan comes to a halt and I climb out, the heat and smell of the small village hitting me like a ton of bricks. I shift my gun and flak, turning my face up to the glare of the sun, waiting as the Marines file out of the vehicles and Uclid comes up on my right. Looking to the Lieutenant in charge I ask, "Which way, sir?"

"You and Uclid are coming with me and my team." He nods for us to follow him and just like normal, we do, following authority and never questioning. A handful of Grunts fall in line behind us as we weave through a tight alley, stepping over a passed out and maybe even dead huddled mass of man, coming out into a bustling market on the other side.

The stands are selling everything from fruit and rugs, to clothing and half rotten meat. The idea of poverty never really hit me until I witnessed three toddlers wrestling over a moldy loaf of bread. Don't get me wrong, I know there are homeless and poor everywhere, I never had anything handed to me growing up, but I had never seen anything up close and personal until my first deployment. The sick and dying huddling together, trying to stay warm at night even though it's stifling hot out during the day. Kids stealing a bag of rotting fruit to feed their family of ten or more. It opens your eyes when you see it in person.

The smells always bother me the most whenever we patrol and as we stay in group, I turn my gaze to my buddy Elliot. The man has been riding my ass the last couple of days, saying I need to get it together. I need to put her behind me, for now. Right now his lectures seem irrelevant as I see him entertaining a handful of kids with a yo-yo he pulls from his vest. I contain a chuckle and shake my head as the kids laugh and gather around him.

I scan the street around us again, taking in the body language and voices of those closest to me. We aren't looking for anything specific, just making our presence known. The higher ups like to keep the locals informed as to whom is in control, when we really aren't in control. Straining and trying to decipher what I know of Arabic I can make out parts of the conversation of two women standing at the kiosk of clothing closest to me, arguing over whether or not red was the right color and I laugh lightly to myself. They don't even seem to care that we are here.

I can see one of the groups 'terms', our nickname for interpreter, up a couple of spaces conversing with a group of men. The same old questions with the same old answers. *Have you seen anything? Do you know where the IED's are?* It turns my stomach as the men shake their heads, denying any knowledge; when I know that they would just as soon rather kill us right here, right now. Don't get me wrong, there are those who are thankful that we are here, but the majority dislikes us. They look at us like monsters, disturbing their way of life. We are just mere tyrants to them.

They don't want us here as much as some of us dislike being here. It's our job. This is what we do, what we love to do, and we just suck it up and do it. We take their nasty looks, muttered curses, and thrown rocks in stride. We learn what really means the most in life and when we get back to the states, we live it up. We cherish the friendships that were just every day occurrences before. We connect with those friends from the past and don't hesitate to make new ones. Being here changes you.

*"We got something over here, Lieutenant,"* I hear come over the radio and I snap out of my musing. We all stop what we're doing, waiting for instructions with our guns at the ready, scanning the crowd. The other team is three streets over already, meandering their way through abandoned buildings that are marked for inspection. The LT waves me forward and I nod to Uclid, seeing him hand off the cheap little yo-yo to one of the little boys he was playing with.

The Grunts fall into line and we make it back to the Hummers in less than a minute, getting in and roaring off to meet up with the others. As we pass a group of children, they smile and wave with one hand, yelling for us to throw them candy or coins. When we don't they pull out the other hand that was behind their backs and whip rocks at our passing vehicles. "Damn demon kids," I hear the Lieutenant issue and a few of the Marines laugh, but I just shake my head. I'm so sick of this place.

Weaving through the crowds of people and dodging the darting children and dogs makes what would have been a minute march into a two minute drive as the grunt driving swears and yells at everything and everyone in his way. Over the radio as we pull up in front of the building where the other team is located I can hear the members describing a suspicious group of locals to the lieutenant.

"Sounds like just a bunch of guys trying to get away from their women," jokes Uclid as our boots hit the dirt, the rancid smell of urine and rotting garbage hitting my nose as I make my way around the front of the vehicle to stand beside the LT.

"At least they have a woman," one of the Marines jabs back and everyone, including me, laughs. Elliot swears at all of us, throwing out a handful of insults ending in a rib on me about Ellie, but I just laugh it off.

"Heads together, boys," the lieutenant orders and we all go silent, straight into combat mode. One mistake, one slip up can mean you or your buddy's life, so when in an un-known situation we need to be on our toes. Taking up a position behind the LT and in front of Uclid, I follow the snake pattern into the building, my M4 tight to my shoulder.

Checking the rooms in formation as we get to the other team is like clockwork. Check the corners. Check behind the doors. Keep your eyes and ears open with your wits about you. Passing a large graffiti covered wall and weaving to my right we meet up with the other Marines, who have seven kneeling Afghan males before them. They are all facing the far wall, chattering amongst themselves.

"What ya got, KK?" the lieutenant asks one of the men as I survey the room, peeking out the windows and seeing the street below. Standing just down the street are three men, talking close together, looking and making arm gestures up to where we are. It makes me think. It makes that ever-present skeptical bone itch in my body and I turn to face the room again.

As the terms question the men, Uclid and I stand in the hall joking back and forth with some of the grunts. "Yeah, well Timmons here has been 'ga-ga' over this girl back home," Uclid jabs at me and I mock chop him in the neck. "He's got it so bad that half the time he can't function." As all of them laugh I look back to the kneeling men and note how nervous one of them looks. He's sweating profusely.

"Yeah, well at least I have a prospect," I puff out my chest, sticking a verbal knife in the always open wound of Elliot's love life, or rather lack thereof. They joke and jab, but their banter fades as I focus back in on that one man. His scraggly beard is dusted with dirt and his clothes are tattered and torn, filthy through and through. The sweat is just pouring down his forehead as his dark brown eyes dart from right to left, not staying put for more than ten seconds at a time. The others aren't sweating as bad as him. There's something up.

As I step closer into the room, only an arm's length away from Uclid and the grunts, I hear the most un-mistakable sound ever. It's like a baseball being hit with a metal bat, but muffled. The air seems to thicken, and as I look at the ground I hear the first *"Grenade!"* alert; spotting the round orb only a step away.

I'm not thinking about me, the grenade is close to Uclid. Not caring where I am in relation to the explosive, I plant both of my hands on Elliot's vest, shoving back as hard as I can. He's one of my best friends. He's my team mate.

I can see him falling back as the flash of light fills my vision. Pain shoots up my leg and through my back as bits and pieces of debris pelt the back of my neck and face. I can feel myself being thrown through the air, then hitting something hard and unyielding. My ears are ringing. High pitched sounds and screaming, making my head feel like it's vibrating fill my worls. I'm numb. I'm cold. Everything is dark.

I hope Uclid is okay.

~~~~

*Ellie*

*Virginia Beach*

"Who the hell opens a nightclub on a Sunday?" I complain as Melody shoves a few more pins into my hair, trying to tame the short locks into an elaborate display that I had tried to protest. Sitting in the massive bathroom of Marco's Virginia Beach penthouse, I look into the mirror to see her push one more pin into place and then hear her sigh in happiness.

"Marco Patuli does, Hun." She smiles, tapping me on the shoulder and telling me to get up from the stool. Standing and stretching, I spy the dress I'm supposed to wear and let out a moan of displeasure. Melody taps me on the butt as she takes the stool to do her makeup and I slump into the huge bedroom, pulling the designer dress from the bed.

It is royal blue, three quarter length sleeved and covered (and I mean covered) in sequins. I can just tell it's going to be itchy, and as I unzip the side so that I can pull it on without damaging it, my dislike of the dress grows. It's a short dress to begin with, but it has a slit up the right thigh. As I shimmy it up into place, tugging on the zipper, I notice the slit comes all the way up to my hip bone. Guess I won't be doing too much sitting tonight, and if I do I'm going to have to remember to angle myself to the right.

"Besides, we don't have to work tomorrow," I hear Mel mumble from the bathroom and I nod to myself, silently agreeing. Looking at myself in the full length mirror, I gently run my fingers over my dark hair, smoothing out a few flyaway strands. Then I lean in close to make sure my blue-green eyes are framed just the way I like them in liner and shadow. Finally, I smooth out the sequins in the dress by running my hand down over my hips, doing a turn and sighing heavily. Slipping into the matching stilettos Marco had set out, I click my way back into the bathroom; getting a whistle from Mel.

"Okay, but I'm probably going to take a cab back before either of you. I still have a headache." I rub my temples, trying to ease the slight pounding. Sure, I was playing it up for a little more than it really was, but they don't need to know that.

I'd rather be back in my bed on this Easter evening than going to a club at eleven o'clock. I had gotten up early and gone to church with Rhea, Chad, and little Charlie, then had a nice lunch at their house with Dana, Kendall, and Harlan. I'm exhausted.

"Oh stop you're belly achin' and take this," Melody gripes, holding her hand out to me with her perfectly manicured bright pink nails. I give her a raised eyebrow in return and she bumps her mocha skin into mine, prying my hand open and dropping two tiny pills in my palm. Staring down at the little pink tablets, I look back up at her with my mouth open, ready to question her.

"Just take them and be quiet." She smiles, returning to applying her makeup. "They'll make the headache go away."

"Are they aspirin?" I ask, still not wanting to put these strange looking things in my mouth. I'm not saying that I don't trust my friend and co-worker, but I know she's into some drugs and I'm not feeling that. As I bring my palm up to get a closer look, the two little pills look more and more like generic baby aspirin, easing my nerves that had spiked at first.

"Yeah. Aspirin," she mumbles as she slides bright red lipstick across her lips, rubbing them together and giving a loud pop as she inspects them in the mirror.

As she runs her pinky along the edge of her bottom lip she looks at me out of the corner of her eye, pushing a small glass of water my way on the countertop. "Well? Go on and stop complainin'."

"Alright, alright," I mumble, sticking my tongue out at her as I take the pills, drinking the glass of water as she babbles on about the new club Marco is opening tonight. I just wander back out into the bedroom and plant myself on the edge of the bed, waiting for her to finish.

Marco's new club is named 'Legacy Lounge' and is situated right on the beach amongst other clubs and restaurants. In the advertisements it stated that it is '*the hottest place in town*' offering '*top bottle service and exquisite décor*'. It has one of the largest dance floors in the area, as well as an enormous horseshoe shaped bar. Melody and I had stopped in earlier, letting Marco know we were heading to his penthouse, but he was too busy running around like a crazy person, bossing everyone around. He spared us kisses on the cheek and enough time to hand us the keys and then he was off again, yelling and shouting, rolling up the sleeves of his European tailored dress shirt.

"Alright, girl, you ready to dance the night away?" Melody smiles and I take in her outfit. Since she's taller than I am, the six inch heels she has on are making her tower over me, the bright red of her skin tight dress reflecting off of the light colors of the bedroom. She gives me a little spin and I just laugh at her. Her pastel pink hair is curled and pinned to the side, studded with the jeweled hair pins Marco had set out with her outfit. That's another good thing about Marco. He knows how to pick out clothes to make us look damn good.

Down into the ornately decorated front room, I spy the car waiting for us at the curb. Right on time. Yet another reliable and great thing about my boss.

Grabbing my little clutch and sharing the hallway mirror with Mel as we do one last makeup check, we take each other's hands and laugh about the night to come on the way out to the black Lincoln Town car. The lights of the Virginia Beach scene pass us by as we immerse ourselves in the bottle of Dom Perignon that was chilled and waiting for us. My headache seems to be going away, even though, like I said, it wasn't as bad as I had played it up to be, but I'm still thankful that it's leaving.

I know Bobby's apartment is somewhere nearby; we had talked about it once. Sitting and listening to Melody sing along with the radio, I zone out and can't help but think of him. His killer smile that seems to make my knees weak even now just thinking about it. His awesome hazel eyes that looked at me out of amazement the night of the party when I climbed into bed with him. I can feel the smile creep onto my lips when I think about how good it felt to have him hold me and the way I had to fight the urge to tilt my head up and meet his lips with mine when I felt them touch my hair.

As we pull up to the curb I can see the spotlights spinning into the night air and the lines of people waiting to get into the new 'Legacy Lounge'. I feel like a rock-star when an usher opens the car door and helps us out, having us wrap our arms around his as he leads us past the large lines, the velvet rope, and through two large glass paneled doors. Just like Marco's style, the doors are inlaid with gold leaf, spelling out the name and covering the handles.

The music is pounding throughout the club, shutting off any chance of talking normally to Melody as the usher leaves us at the coat check. Looking to my friend, a giddy little smile splays across both of our faces as we take in the packed scene. Marco has outdone himself, again. I think this club might even rival his Las Vegas one, and as I hand the man my clutch, taking a ticket in return, I turn in a slow circle surveying the room. Red, blue and purple are the dominant colors played across the walls and floor in fabulous patterns, along with swirling through the air from the lights above.

Mel takes my hand again, leading me through the dancing and talking crowds to the bar. During our visit earlier it had just looked normal, but now in the lowered lights it is fantastic. Lighted from underneath, the gold tones glow as if it is on fire. The bar top has lighted tiles embedded into the wood, changing and flickering with the music tying the bar to the dance floor effortlessly. As Mel leans over close to the bartender, ordering us only God knows what, I can't help but look out onto the dance floor and want to be out there. *"I'll get the chance,"* I tell myself and turn back to accept the drink from my friend.

We chat and run through our first drinks in no time, turning back to the bartender and ordering another as I feel hands come around my waist. Thinking it is Marco, I just lean back as the white dress shirt clad arms encircle my waist. I know it's not Marco when a scruffy chin brushes against my ear and the deep, smooth voice whispers in my ear, "Well, fancy seein' you here, darlin'."

Spinning around, almost spilling my drink, I come nose to nose with the smiling Garth Cobb, releasing a breath I didn't know I was holding. I kiss his cheek over the scar that runs across his face and look right into those gorgeous green eyes of his. He winks, a heart melting grin caressing his lips, and I hug him tight to me.

"What the hell are you doin' here, cowboy?" I say into his ear, spotting his boyfriend, Brad Muncy, weaving his way through the crowd toward us.

"We needed to see this new hot spot." He laughs, his hands still at my waist holding me to him as Brad wraps me in a hug just as tight. I introduce them to Mel, putting their drinks on our tab that Marco had in place for us, and we settle into a VIP area reserved for only us.

These two guys have been so welcoming to me since I found Rhea last summer. As I sit between them on the velvet couch, Garth throws his arm around my shoulders as Brad puts his hand on my knee. A normal position for these two. They are always overly touchy-feely, but it's okay with me. Besides they aren't interested in what I have to offer, anyway.

The music pumps away as we're served another round of drinks, Melody obviously flirting away with Brad as Garth and I are lost in conversation about my favorite little guy, my 'nephew' Charlie. My headache is totally gone and I'm feeling rather good, actually having to fight off the urge to have Brad move his hand up my leg further, which is weird, but I just shake it off and carry on talking to Garth as he runs his fingers over the back of my neck. It feels so good that at one point I catch myself leaning into his touch and slap him in the chest as he chuckles.

"Well, here's my two favorite girls," Marco's

familiar voice rings out over the music and I turn to see his tall, muscular frame leaning over to kiss Mel on the cheek. I have to bite down the urge to tip over from moving my head so fast and slightly shake myself out of it, feeling woozy.

"Looks like Ellie here is already tipsy." He laughs, kissing my cheek and whispering, "And who are these two fellas?"

I try to introduce them calmly, but as I'm telling him where I know Brad and Garth from, Brad squeezes my knee and a lightning bolt of desire shoots through me, stopping my words mid-sentence. As Marco gives me a strange look, his lips quirk up in a smile and he shares a look with Melody, getting me to question what they are laughing at.

"Let me borrow my friend here," Marco says to Garth and Brad as he takes my hand, pulling me to my feet and out closer to the bar. "Did Melody happen to give you some pills, little girl?" he says in my ear, the feel of his breath on my skin making it tingle and my breath catching in my chest. *What is wrong with me? What was in those drinks?* I think to myself, answering Marco with a 'yes'. I'm confused at the burst of laughter that leaves him, his dark brown eyes smiling down at me as he apologizes to those around us for disturbing them.

"Well, girl," he laughs some more and I hit him on the arm, "it looks like Mel slipped you some Molly."

"Who's Molly?" I ask as my words slur together and I wobble slightly in my heels. What the hell is he talking about? I don't know anyone named Molly.

"It's not a 'who', silly girl, but a 'what'." He smiles again, wrapping my shoulders in his strong arms as he leads me back to the table. I still have no freaking idea what he is talking about as he plops me back down between Brad and Garth, leaning in to whisper one more thing after kissing my cheek. "Molly is ecstasy. Have fun." He laughs, waving a quick goodbye before disappearing into the writhing bodies out on the dance floor.

Is he serious? I can't seem to make any sense of the thoughts rolling around in my head right now as Garth's lips touch my cheek. "You wanna dance, Hun?" He smiles and I can't help but nod my head yes. I shouldn't want to dance or be close to Brad and Garth; I should want to beat the hell out of Melody for giving me drugs. I should want to rip every strand of pastel pink hair out of her head and slap her in the face with it, but instead I follow Garth out onto the packed dance floor, flanked by Brad.

I lose track of time and of myself as the music plays on, the three of us dancing and grinding out on the middle of the floor. I should tell them about the drugs, but soon enough I don't remember what it was that Marco has told me and I'm lost in the feeling of their attention. Their hands on my hips. Garth's lips on my neck. Brad's fingers running up my thigh, pushing my dress up slowly.

Wait, what am I doing? I shouldn't be doing this, but it feels too good right now. The next thing I know, we're outside the club walking down the sidewalk.

"Where are we goin'?" I laugh, trying to keep up with Garth, who is pulling me forward and Brad, who has his arms wrapped around my waist, his lips seemingly attached to my ear as he nibbles on it, sending the shivers across my skin. I shouldn't be doing this, I remind myself again but everything is a little hazy.

"We have a hotel room right down here." Garth laughs, his green eyes lighting up as his eyebrows waggle at me. Brad sweeps me up in his arms and I snuggle into his shoulder, giggling as his lips touch mine, his tongue running along the sensitive skin. I feel him stumble, evidence of his slightly inebriated state and I laugh right along with him as he kisses me again.

The beeping of a key-card being slid, the clicking of the door locking behind us, and a few seconds later I'm dropping that designer dress down to the floor. Standing before the two men, I'm not really comprehending what I'm doing. I only know that their lips on my skin feels amazing right now. The way their hands roam over my skin and pull me down onto the bed with them makes my heart race.

I'm not thinking about the possible consequences. I'm not thinking about Bobby.

~~~~

Ellie

*April 1, 2013*

My head is pounding, my body hurts everywhere,

and as I gather my dress and shoes from last night off the hotel room floor I'm hating myself. How could I have done that? I know it was fueled by the ecstasy Melody had slipped me and the alcohol I had consumed, but there is no excuse for sleeping with Garth and Brad. I could have said no, but the words never formed on my lips.

"Leavin' so soon, darlin'?" Garth asks from the bathroom doorway, his half naked form wet from the shower with his green eyes washing over me. Pulling the dress over my head, I try to give him a smile but I know it's weak and he shakes his head. "We were all pretty drunk last night, darlin'. There's nothin' to be ashamed of."

"What am I goin' to tell Bobby?" I whisper, plopping down onto the edge of the messy bed to slip my heels on. It's what I've been thinking about all morning. What am I going to say to Bobby? Should I tell him? I have to tell him. I'll have to tell him everything in order for us to be truly happy. He'd have to know who he's getting involved with.

"Well," Garth ponders my question for a second, sitting down next to me, "you'll know when the time is right to tell him. It'll be one of those moments when you're just joking about your past and then the conversation will turn to sexual partners. Trust me, I've heard some stories about that boy that could rival Hugh Hefner, so he has no grounds to get mad." He chuckles and kisses my cheek.

It doesn't make me feel any better. In fact, I feel horrible. How could I have let this happen? I keep kicking myself in the ass mentally as I say goodbye to Brad and Garth, leaving their hotel room and getting in the first cab that pulls up. I don't try and hide the shame filled tears that flow on the ride to Marco's penthouse, only wiping them away with a shaky hand as I step from the cab, paying the man and not waiting for the change.

"Well, look who decided to grace us with her presence," Marco jabs as I make my way through his kitchen, not bothering to look them in the eye, I head for the upstairs bathroom. I can hear their footsteps following me up the stairs, but I don't stop.

I don't want to talk about it. Slamming the door shut, I crank on the shower, almost ripping the dress from my body and chucking the heels into the garbage can out of anger. The tears and shame take over and I fall to my knees, naked and crying in the middle of the enormous bathroom.

I hate myself. Again. I hate that I couldn't keep my legs closed. I hate that I couldn't say no when I needed to. I hate that I keep fucking up my life whenever things seem to start going in the right direction.

I feel Marco's strong arms surrounding me and pulling me from the tile floor, holding me to his chest as he whispers in my ear, "Tell me what's wrong, Hun." Melody's touch meets my shoulder and I swing out of anger at her.

"You lied," I sob, pointing my finger in her face.

"Yeah, well, I thought you needed to loosen up." She shrugs, sinking back against the sink cabinet. *Really?* Is that all she has to say for the reason she gave me ecstasy and lying about it?

Shaking my anger away, I divulge my night to my boss and co-worker all the while still lying naked in Marco's arms. They keep silent. Too silent and I pull myself from Marco's arms, standing and wrapping myself in a towel.

"The only thing I can say, Hun, is maybe… to not let it bother you." He stands and leans back against the sink, his muscular arms crossed over his chest. "You and Bobby aren't even together. Yeah, sure, you're 'talking'," he says with air quotes, "but we're not in high school anymore. You're a grown woman. You can sleep with whomever you want."

"Yeah, but I feel as if I betrayed him," I say, wiping the last tears from my cheek. Marco just shrugs, throwing his arm over my shoulder, and kisses my temple. I can hear my phone ringing in the bedroom and Melody comes back in, her hand outstretched so I can see that it's Rhea calling.

I really don't feel like talking to her right now, my heart is still hurting from my monumental mistake, but I answer it anyway. "Ellie," she says, not even waiting for me to say a full hello, and I can tell she's been crying.

"Rhea, what's wrong? Is Charlie okay?" My mood goes from bad to worse in a split second, my chest tightening with hundreds of scenarios playing out in my mind right now. Is he sick? Is it Chad?

"It's Bobby," she cries and I can hear Chad talking in the background. Bobby. My breath catches in my chest and I wait to hear what she has to say.

*Hurt?* Bobby? I can't take it. The pressure on my chest explodes. I'm a horrible person. Pushing that all aside, I pray to God and hope that he listens even after my actions last night. *"Please, not Bobby."*

# CHAPTER 5

## BOBBY

*April 20, 2013*

There are two hundred and ten ceiling tiles in my room. You want to know how I know this? Because it's all I've been staring at for the last week since being flown back to the states. Stark, white, boring, God damn hospital ceiling tiles. The door to my room opens and I avert my eyes from the same spot

I've been looking at since waking up to see the plump middle aged nurse waddle her way into my room, a clipboard in hand.

"How are you feelin' this morning, Mr. Timmons?" she asks, just like she has every day, working her pencil across her page as she checks my IV and monitors.

"How would you feel if you lost half of your leg to a grenade?" I grumble. It's the same answer I've always given her and she huffs, giving me an angry look out of the corner of her eye.

Well? What does she want me to say? *Oh, I feel great even though I'm missing my left leg below the knee.* Yeah.

"The doctor says you'll be back in therapy this afternoon. I have to check your bandages before you go." She nods toward my bed, asking me silently to remove the blanket from my leg, but I don't move. I don't want to look at it. She huffs again and puts her clipboard down on the bedside table, pulling the sheet from my leg and I move my eyes back up to the ceiling.

Waking up in the hospital after the explosion I was so confused. Uclid was there at my side and I'm glad he's okay. I hadn't thought I was hurt too bad, looking to my friend and joking with him about why he looked so glum with this sad look on his face. He broke the news to me like a bowling ball smashing through a china cabinet, dealing with my explosion of anger afterward as I ripped the blanket from my body; seeing the injury myself for the first time.

I can't help but feel as if my life is over. My life as a SEAL is definitely over. I'll never run like I used to, enjoying the feel of my muscles working away. I'll never be the same man. Sure, there are those that have carried on with their team career with an injury like mine, but right now I can't see myself doing it.

"Come on now, Mr. Timmons. You have to watch me so you can do this yourself." The nurse tugs on my shirt and I turn my eyes to her, not moving my arms. She tugs on my shirt again and I sigh heavily, shifting in the bed and throwing my right leg over the edge, waiting for her to start her demonstration. I know how to change a dressing, but I'll let her amuse me for a few minutes.

The sight of my leg disgusts me. It's red and irritated, not to mention sore. As she pulls the last bandage away I have to grind my teeth to keep the string of curses from spilling out. Of course I have friends who have lost fingers or limbs and have run into service men and women who have, but facing this myself is another story. Being the one with the bandages is different. I never thought this would happen. Sure, being a SEAL, the danger comes hand in hand, but I just didn't think it would happen. It pisses me off to no end.

The nurse is fumbling with the roll of gauze and the pain in my chest boils over in anger. "Give me that," I snap and yank the roll from her hand, ignoring the shocked look on her face.

Twirling the damn material around the stump of what once was my shin, the hurt continues to build, tightening my chest as tears waver on the edge from spilling over. I am not going to cry, at least not in front of this pudgy woman. All I need is for her to go out and gossip about the hard ass that broke down in front of her.

After finishing the bandage, I pull the suspension sleeve over it, tugging it up to hit over my knee while ignoring the ache from the tender flesh. Sliding the simple prosthetic limb from the bedside, I slide it into place and lower myself into the ready wheelchair. "Okay then," the nurse mumbles, pushing me from the room and heading toward the Physical Therapy wing.

We pass a girl standing in the hall holding flowers in her hands, and for a split second my breathing stops. Is it Ellie? As we pass I get a good look at the woman's face and the sudden hope that had risen in my chest is tampered again by the anger and hurt as I realize it's not her. It's not that pretty little thing that I dream about at night when I actually sleep. I haven't dared to talk to her yet. I don't want her to see me like this.

I have seen Chad and Reno; they've been in to see me a couple of times in the last week. Chad tells me that Ellie is calling and texting Rhea every chance she gets, asking for updates on me. I just can't keep it together long enough to see her right now. I feel like I'm less than a man. Chad has been telling me that seeing those who care about me will bring a better mood into my situation right now. I just can't. I don't want to see those questioning and pitying looks in their eyes.

An hour and a half later, I'm walking with the help of support bars gripped between either of my hands as my therapist's hands are on my hips, the sweat dripping from my forehead with the pain radiating through my leg. I don't want to stop. I want to walk and get the hell out of here. I don't want this damn silver leg with the sneaker attached. I don't want this pain.

"Alright then, Bobby, that's enough," my therapist

says as I reach the end of the walkway and swing around into the waiting wheelchair. The reconstructed muscles in my leg are screaming and I pull the prosthetic off, hoping for some relief which doesn't come.

"You did awesome today, Bobby. Nurse Shelley will take you to the tub, and I'll see you after dinner." My doctor waves goodbye as I nod, leaving the room being wheeled by the next pudgy nurse.

Like really? Can't I have one good looking nurse? No, I'd rather have Ellie. I'd rather have her petite figure, dark short hair, and striking blue-green eyes in my presence. Just thinking of her beautiful face makes me close my eyes, trying to live in the day dream. I feel as if I can even smell her perfume; the fruity, flowery alluring scent that wraps itself around my heart. Maybe Chad is right. Maybe if I see her, I'll feel better.

What will she think? They haven't told her what kind of injury I've suffered, so I wonder what she thinks happened? What if she is disgusted by the half a man that will stand before her? What if this damn metal leg makes her think twice about giving me a chance?

That familiar and seemingly ever present pain in my heart rejoins me as I slide into the therapy tub, letting the soothing temperature and jets sink into my stressed muscles. This nurse is talking to me, but I don't care. I let her words blur into oblivion as I lean my head back on the edge of the massive tub and stare at the ceiling.

Sometimes it feels as if this is unreal, as if it is a dream and I'll wake up at any second. The pain, it isn't real. The hurt in my heart and the hate in my mind for my situation aren't real. I'll wake up in my apartment and be able to call up Ellie, taking her out to dinner and a walk along the beach, feeling the sand under my toes.

But that isn't right. This *is* real. The pain I'm feeling below my left knee from my strained, reconstructed muscles is very much a reality.

One more bandage change after the tub and I'm left in my room, sitting in the wheelchair by the window to look out over the bustling cityscape. Norfolk is as crammed as bread in a can and it makes me want to see the country. I want the little town of Wakefield to be exact. To drive down the almost bare two lanes with the corn and tobacco fields on each side. I want to smell the fresh air after a slight rain, and the dirt on my hands as I help Chad and Harlan put in hay on the farm. I want to be anywhere but here, with my two hundred and ten ceiling tile friends.

"If you stare too long you might creep out the people on the street," the familiar voice pulls me from my loathing and I swing my chair around to see Chief leaning up against the doorway, his new job attire a striking difference to our usual camo.

He's got grey suit pants with black dress shoes, a white shirt and black tie. His suit coat is probably out in his government issued car, courtesy of NCIS. As he saunters in, his leader attitude still firmly intact, I can't help but shake my head at him. Getting married and having a young son still hasn't dampened his cocky aurora.

"Hey Chief, how's it goin'?" I wheel my chair over to my bed, hopping out as Chad sits down on the corner of the hospital white sheets, throwing his feet up in the spare stiff chair. Tucking my leg under the thin sheet, I can see him watching me out of the corner of his eye. I can't blame him. I'd be curious too if our roles were reversed.

"I'm same as always. The bigger question is how *you* are?" He gives me a strong look, assessing me with those blue eyes that used to cut through me when we were in training and on missions. Sometimes I can read Chief just by his eyes, and I can tell he's waiting for me to tell him that I'm having a hard time. He can probably tell and I don't try and hide my disdain any further, sighing heavily and leaning back against my pillows.

"It's hard," I mumble, seeing his eyebrows raise and his head nod in agreement. Hard isn't even close. Impossible, that is a better word, but I can't admit total defeat. Admitting defeat would kill what little piece of my SEAL self I have left and I'm clinging to that for dear life. I need that piece of me to get through this shit.

I can tell he's waiting for me to go on and elaborate as he straightens his tie, clearing his throat lightly and peeking at me from the corner of his eye. He was never one to push unless it was necessary. He knows when to back off and leave well enough alone. That's what made him a good leader and a good Chief.

"I don't feel like me," I have to force out between clenched teeth, the muscles in my jaw tight from the pain in my chest. It hurts even more to admit it out loud. To say the words and realize that this is my life now, there is no going back. As my fists clench at my sides and I focus in on my tattooed forearm I say, "I don't want this to be me."

"But it is you, Bobby," Chad says through a heavy

sigh, slapping his hand on my shoulder and looking me right in the eye. "I can't say that I know what you're goin' through and I can't tell you what to feel, but I don't want to see you like this." He waves his hand at my slouching figure, and I feel the need to sit up straight while being scrutinized by him.

"I need you to see the doctors they want you to see. They can help with the mental aspect of your injury," he sternly adds, giving me a knowing look. Word must have trickled down that I had refused to see the psychologist. I don't want them to tell me that I need to take this drug and that drug to feel better. I don't want to feel like a zombie in life.

"I don't need to take God damn drugs, Chief," I snap, throwing the blanket off of my leg and pointing to it. "I need my damn leg back!" I can feel the heat reaching my skin, turning my neck and face red. The anger that I've been trying to hold back feels like it's going to rip through my chest like an Alien as I stare at my friend, Chad. My one time Chief. My one time and never to be again SEAL brother.

"Snap out of it, Timmons," he raises his voice, his blue eyes baring down on me as he stands, moving to the side of the bed. "You're not the only damn man who's been through this. This happens every day and whether you want to admit it or not, being a SEAL, you go out there knowing that this is a possible outcome because that's what we do." His stare is trying to force the truth into my mind and I turn my face away, looking out the window and trying to not be here.

The hurt and reality of my life is pressing down on my chest, taking my breathing to heavy and labored as I fight the tears that try and take over. I'm not a bitch,

I don't want to cry. I'm focusing in on the sounds of the city outside my sterile hospital room when Chad's fist connects with my chest, taking my breath away and spilling my anger over the edge it was teetering on.

"What the hell do you want me to say, Chief?" I yell, turning on him in full blown rage mode, grabbing his dress shirt in my hands and balling the material in clenched fingers. "What. The. Fuck. Do you want me to do? Tell you I don't want to live like this, because I don't. I don't want to be the man kids stare at as I walk down the street. I don't want to be the friend that everyone pities. Fuck that." I shove him back, wiping at the stream of moisture running down my heated cheeks and seeing the turmoil run over Chad's face.

"No one is going to pity you, Bobby," he yells right back, getting only inches away from my face, poking his finger into my chest. "You need to realize that you're a hero. You saved the lives of your SEAL brother and over ten Grunts. They would have died if you hadn't stepped up. Don't you realize that?" He steps back and scrapes his hand back through his graying hair, scratching over his beard as I can tell he's trying to rein in his anger.

The door to my room opens a crack and the pudgy nurse from this morning pokes her head in, barely getting out a *"Is everything okay in here"* before both Chad and I yell at her to get out and she disappears in a hurry. I know he'll apologize for that when he leaves. As he turns back to face me, I take a deep breath, trying to let his words sink in. I don't feel like a hero.

Sitting back down on the corner of my bed, he

rests his hand on my shoulder. "Just please see the doctor, Bobby; they are only here to help." He squeezes my shoulder, giving me a small smile and he sighs when I nod my head, silently agreeing. I know I need to talk to them; I just don't want to admit that I need help.

"I've already talked to the therapist that helped Rhea with her shoulder and leg and he's willing to help you." He stands, fixing his shirt and shoving his hands in his pocket. "Plus I thought it would be a good idea if you came to live with me and Rhea when you're released."

"What?" I ask, trying not to choke on the words as my surprise at his statement spills out. Is he serious? "Why would you want me to move in with you and Rhea when I have a perfectly good apartment to live in?"

"Your apartment is on the second floor, and if you have been listening to what your doctors have been tellin' ya, you woulda realized that goin' up and down stairs too much isn't recommended." He gives me a raised eyebrow, and I nod my head, mentally cursing whomever he got his info from. That's Chad. Always able to get what he wants to know.

"And we can make the downstairs bedroom yours. Plus, Ellie has been blowin' Rhea's phone up wondering about you. She knows you want to tell her what happened, but Rhea says she's worried sick over you. Seems like Ellie has become attached to you." He gives me that raised eyebrow, matched with a smirk and I can't help but smile back, letting a slight chuckle run through my chest for the first time in days.

"I'll think about it," I say, resting back against the

pillows. It would be nice to have people around me instead of being alone in my apartment, but I don't want to be a burden.

"Yeah, well," Chad smiles, clapping his hands together and I immediately know he's going to say something I might not like, "I've already hired a moving crew to get your stuff from your apartment, so, you're 'thinking'," he throws up air quotes as I shake my head at him, "is going to have to end in a '*Well yeah, Chief, I'd love to live with you and Rhea. Thanks!*'."

"You're a son of a bitch, you know that?" I laugh at him as he smiles, clapping me on the back again.

"My momma tells me that every day," he jokes.

As we sit and talk, I let the ideas sink in. I'm going to live with my friend Chad. In a quiet, rural area away from all the noise. I'm going to be close to Ellie.

This could work out.

~~~~

*Ellie*

"Where's Chad?" I ask my cousin, Rhea, as she's buckling her squirming son into the back seat of her husband's Silverado. We are on the way to the usual Saturday dinner between Rhea and her friends, this time being held at Kendall and Harlan's place. I love being around everyone at the same time. They always have so much fun, and after the work week I've had, I need some fun for certain.

"He's workin' late I guess." She shrugs, but I can see her spare me a quick look out of the corner of her eye and I know she's lying. I can read Ray-Ray like a book and I wait until she's in the driver's seat to give her the laser-beam of skepticism.

She ignores me with a little effort, evident in the red creeping up her neck, turning her attention to backing out of her garage and heading down the road. "Don't look at me like that, Ellie Mae," she chides.

"Well, don't lie," I tort back, tapping my fingers on the center console as she turns toward town. She's not a good secret holder, especially when the person grilling her knows that she knows, and she squirms slightly under my stare.

I turn into the backseat and smile at little Charlie, taking his foot in my hand and hearing him giggle. "Tell Mommy not to lie to Aunty Ellie," I coo at him and he laughs, causing a grin to reach my ears as I turn back to Rhea.

"Okay," she huffs in frustration, slamming her hand down on the steering wheel as we come to a stop sign. Giving me an annoyed look, she sighs again before starting in. "He's with Bobby in Norfolk."

Bobby. My heart jumps for a second and I have to grip the door handle to try and ease the tension zipping through my body just at the mention of his name. Since Easter, I've felt like my chest might explode at every mention of his name and it's no different now. My mind goes back to the night at Rhea's house and the feel of his skin on mine. The way the warmth seemed to seep into my bones when he kissed my hair.

Being free from any drama with Jake has left me countless hours to day dream about Bobby and my heart has filled every second with fantasies. The way his lips will feel against mine when he finally kisses me for real, hopefully. It will probably make me weak. The ways his strong arms will hold me to him and make me feel safe. I crave it more than I should.

"Is," I choke out and have to stop. Clearing my throat, I look out my window trying to blink back the tears that are trying to leak out.

"Is he okay?" No one will tell me how he was hurt, just that he was and he's healing now. They all shake their heads and tell me that Bobby wants to tell me himself, but I'm dying here trying to prepare myself for what I might face when I see him in person.

Was he shot? Did his hummer hit a roadside bomb? Was he burnt or beaten? I have no idea.

"He's fine," Rhea says softly, patting my knee with her soft, warm hand, making me feel a little better. Her blue-grey eyes try and convey that everything will be okay as she peeks between me and the road, but I need to know for myself.

"When is he going to be well enough to see me?" I feel as if I whine the last word, putting my thumb nail in my mouth and nervously biting away on it. Maybe he doesn't want to see me. That realization hurts and I squeeze my eyes shut as a few tears slide down.

"Actually," Rhea's voice lifts in excitement and I wipe at my cheeks, turning to face her as she pulls down her old street headed toward Kendall's trailer.

She sees my tears and rubs her thumb over my skin, smiling sweetly. "Don't cry, Ell, cuz Bobby is comin' to live with Chad and me when he's released." She smiles wide and I'm dumbstruck.

What did she just say? Bobby? Living with Chad and Rhea? No, she has to be playing some sick joke. "Ray, this isn't funny," I start to say, my tone angry and sharp but she throws her hand up and stops me mid-sentence.

"I know how you feel about him, Ell," she whispers, pulling onto the grass beside Harlan's old Jeep. Turning the engine off, she sighs, flopping back against the seat and turning toward me.

"It's the same way I felt about Chad. You want him so bad it hurts, but you don't know whether or not he wants you back. Every spare second of your time is filled with fleeting fantasies, even when you try not to think of him or haven't thought of him in a while."

She hit the nail on the head, and as she gets out, I rest my head back and try to compose myself as I'm looking up at the grey interior. I do want him so bad it hurts. My chest feels like it's a wet rag being twisted over and over, wringing the life right out of me as if it were mere water.

It scares me to feel like this about someone while still trying to get the divorce papers signed by Jake. I don't want to hurt Bobby in any way. I also don't want Jake to find out I'm seeing anyone when it does come down to it. I'm afraid at what he'll do and get away with, since he's a Trooper and everything seems to 'disappear' when it comes to him.

Opening my eyes and looking out to the doublewide that I remember running around when

Rhea and I were little, I see one way that I might have hurt Bobby already. Garth and Brad are leaning up against the railing on the porch, their eyes on the truck where I'm sitting, and my stomach starts to do backflips. The slam of the back door brings me from my shocked state and I undo my seatbelt with a shaky hand.

I could kick my own ass for twenty four hours straight about what I got myself into with Garth and Brad. I was stupid and careless. Making my way across the grass, I can feel them watching me and I look up to meet Garth's green eyes, that same old killer smile on his lips. At times I'll be sitting alone at home or in the dressing room at Subzero and I'll just beat myself up mentally about that night in Virginia Beach. I can't take it back.

Shaking off the familiar horrible feeling that comes with the thought of telling Bobby about that night, I smile and wave to Garth, Brad, and everyone gathered around the porch. I'll bite the bullet, keeping my word not to let it get to me too much. I'll focus on Bobby and the thought of maybe seeing him soon.

# CHAPTER 6

## BOBBY

*April 30, 2013*

Standing in what is now my empty bedroom, I'm both nervous and anxious to go down the stairs and get into Chad's truck, leaving this apartment to live with him and Rhea while I continue my therapy. The white walls are boring and uninviting and as I pull the shades down over the window, I let the late afternoon darkness sink in. It's a familiar feeling, this loneliness and despair. I've become friends with it over the last couple of weeks.

Moving my eyes down to my left leg, I let out a string of mumbled curses at the metal material and attached sneaker, crumpling the meek curtain that lined my window between my fingers. I've spent countless nights in that hospital bed, lying awake and hating myself with every second. The psychologist that I'm seeing helps, just being there to talk through things, but I've refused the anti-depressants so far. I don't want to take them. I want this hurt in my chest to disappear on its own because I'm a man.

I was a sailor. I was a SEAL. Now, well now I'm just a statistic with a metal leg and few scars on my back. Yeah, sure, they say that I'm a hero, but as of right now I don't feel like one.

I feel like I've let everyone in my life down, especially my SEAL brothers. I feel as if I'm a failure to Chad and Reno, who had mentored me and watched my back, honing me into the SEAL that I was. Even Ellie, who doesn't really know what has happened to me yet. She is waiting for a man, a whole man, to come back and pick up where we left off. All she'll be getting is what scraps are left over.

I can hear Chad and Reno laughing and joking around outside as I take another look around. Pulling the last duffle bag with my clothes from of the bed, gripping my cane tight, I turn to head out. My apartment wasn't anything special, but I have to smirk remembering some of the antics that have gone on here. Like the crazy parties with Uclid and some of our other sailor friends, sometimes being so rowdy that the cops were called by my neighbors. They were good times, but they are gone now. All blown away by the grenade, in that God forsaken hell hole that reeked of urine and decay.

'*No*,' I have to tell myself sternly, stopping in the middle of the living room and shutting my eyes tight, fighting off the urge to scream at my situation. '*No, my life is NOT over. I am still who I was, just changed. I am a good man and an even better sailor. I saved my friends. I'm okay.*' I can hear footsteps coming up the metal stairs outside and I take a deep breath in, trying to calm the rage welling inside me.

"Are ya ready to go, Timmons?" Reno smiles as he looks around the apartment with Chad on his heels. They have done a good job at making sure I have everything essential, wrapping up the furniture and appliances to keep the dust off. Reno's tan skin and dark hair is accented by the khaki cargo shorts and white polo he is sporting and I secretly hate him, wanting his complexion as opposed to my freckles.

"I'm ready," I say, nodding my head and trying not to hobble too much as I follow them to the door. After one last look I pull the door shut, turning the key in the deadbolt while hopefully opening another door in my life with living in Wakefield. I'm praying that at least this opportunity will have a good outcome.

My leg is still sore but manageable, and as my cane clicks on the stairs Chad turns to me and asks, "Need any help?"

It's a simple question, but it stings. With a shake of my head I bite back a nasty reply, averting my eyes to my feet while fighting this anger brewing in my chest. I shouldn't need anyone to ask me if I need fucking help getting down the stairs, but I guess it comes with the new territory.

Throwing my duffle into the back of Chad's truck, I climb into the passenger seat as my two friends talk about the route they are going to take back to the house, but I'm not listening. I throw my head back against the headrest, letting some of the anger roll through my arms as I ball my fists repeatedly. Looking down at my forearms, I watch as my tattooed flesh contracts and releases.

Then I look again at my left knee; I hate that apparatus below it so much. I adjust my shorts to try and hide the tan suspension sleeve, knowing that it's impossible and the anger within makes my breathing speed up. I want my leg back.

"You okay?" Chad's voice shocks me and I turn on him, knowing my anger is still displayed all over my face. His eyes lock onto mine and he slowly shuts his door, silently waiting for me to explode. I take the opportunity and let out a loud, seemingly earth shattering yell, pounding my fists on the dashboard and feeling the truck shake in the aftermath. I can feel my skin flushing, the heat making sweat break out under my t-shirt as I pound my left hand on the center console while gritting my teeth.

I can't look at Chad for a minute after that and as we sit in silence, my heavy breathing is the only noise between us. It felt good to let it out, but the hurt starts to set in again, tightening my chest and feeling as if it might squeeze my heart right out of my body. Casting my eyes to the side I see Chad leaned back, waiting like the silent and strong man that he is.

"Sorry 'bout that," I say, my breathing still heavy as I slide the seatbelt across my torso, snapping it into place as my hands throb from the abuse I just put them through. My therapist says that I should start doing the kickboxing and running like I used to, to let off steam and focus my energy on healing. I should probably start listening to them to try and keep this from happening again, but it's easier said than done when you have to lie in bed each morning and tell yourself repeatedly to get up, that life isn't over.

"It's okay, Bobby." Chad smiles lightly, pulling out behind Reno's Jeep headed toward the highway. "Anytime you wanna talk," he mumbles, clearing his throat and trying not to sound too sentimental but still meaning it. He gives me a sidelong glance while merging into traffic.

I nod, giving him a silent acknowledgment to taking him up on his offer and he focuses back on the road. I know he means it, but I don't think I'm really ready to talk over everything that I'm feeling right now. Maybe in a little while.

The ride is pretty much silent after that, except when Chad boasts about Rhea's cooking which I already know is good, so I agree right along with him adding my two cents when he asks about my favorite foods. I laugh with him as he gushes about Charlie and am happy to see him loving his life. I almost forget about my situation until we turn onto his road and I shift in my seat, the tight muscles in my left leg screaming at me and bringing me back to reality.

I sigh heavily as Chad puts the truck in park, giving me a sympathetic look as he runs his hand back through his greying hair. The front door to his home opens and Rhea steps out with Charlie on her hip, waving and smiling at us, lifting my spirits.

"Don't worry, man," he says, punching me in the shoulder like he always does and whispers, "things will get better."

"Yeah," I mumble, gripping my cane and slowly opening my door, fearing that first look on Rhea's face. I try and smile at her approaching figure as my sneakers hit the grass. Seeing her eyes flit from my face to my leg, I hold my breath.

Her look only lasts a second before her eyes meet mine displaying happiness without the usual trace of sympathy I've come accustom to from the nurses and it makes me happy. As she throws her arm around my shoulder, hugging me and telling me she's happy I'm here, I genuinely smile for the first time in a couple of days. It's not laced with sadness, just a smile.

With my cane in my left hand I take Charlie, cooing and drooling, from Rhea as she insists on helping her husband and Reno carry some of my things into their house. Up the front steps and through their front hallway, I am feeling better by the second just being surrounded by their presence. Charlie is pulling at the neck of my t-shirt and trying to squirm down as Rosa joins us, her daughter Marisol on her hip. She wraps me in a tight hug as well, taking the baby from me and telling me to sit down.

I like this, it feels good. Their smiling faces and happy voices make me grin. This is better than sitting alone in my apartment that's for sure. As they joke and harass each other, throwing my bags into the spare bedroom, I can't help but laugh at them, joining in when I can and harassing Chief most of all. He takes it in stride like he always does, laughing it off with throwing a few ribs my way as I sit at the kitchen table facing the front door, my hand rubbing at my left thigh and knee subconsciously.

Chad had been right about going up and down those stairs at my apartment building; my leg is killing me now. Doing the loading of the truck, I was confident that I'd be fine, but now, I could go for an ice pack. An ice pack that weighs five pounds and will encompass my entire leg would be ideal, but I won't let it bother me.

"Do you need anything?" Rhea's voice breaks my concentration, and I snap out of my musing to see that I'm staring blankly ahead at her and Rosa, standing at the door of what will be my bedroom. Her blue-grey eyes sneak down to my hand rubbing at my leg and I curse myself silently, moving it away quickly to brush it through my hair and rest on the back of my neck. I know she's just concerned, but I'm just not use to it yet.

I shake my head. "No I'm fine," I lie, shifting the pant leg of my shorts to try and hide the suspension sleeve again, but it's pointless. I can still see her looking at me out of the corner of my eye and I turn to try and give her a sweet smile. Seeing hers in return, I nod my head, silently telling her that I'm okay and she returns to her conversation with Rosa, both with a child on their hip.

Rhea's short stature and caring attitude make me think of Ellie and my chest starts to hurt for another reason. I wonder if they told her I'd be moving in today. I should have called her and told her I'd be here, but I didn't. I had wanted to, grabbing my cell and bringing her info up on the screen probably thirty times. Each time I closed it out, not pushing the 'call' button, not hearing her voice or telling her what had happened and kicking myself in the ass later on for being so weak. I don't want her to see me like this with my cane and having to sit after only a little bit of physical activity.

"You know, Timmons," Reno smiles, pulling the chair out beside me and plopping down into it with a thud while slapping his hand on my back, "you have too much clothing." He laughs, joined by Chad who straddles the chair to my right while handing me a bottle of water. "I think you and Rosa should go in competition and see who has more shirts, because I think you might win."

"Hey," I smile and can't help but join in on their laughter, "you can never have too many shirts. You never know when you'll need a casual or dressy one." They laugh even harder at me, their faces turning red and I go along. It feels good to laugh, to let it out. As Rhea and Rosa join us with the babies, I've laughed so hard that my chest hurts in a good way.

The group of us settles into comfortable, normal conversation as Rhea and Rosa work on dinner. The three of us shift the kids between us and it's almost as if this is home. I start to feel a family feeling again, I don't feel alone. I know that this is going to be a long road. I'm hoping that dark feeling doesn't make it an impossible road.

While helping Chad set the table, my head snaps toward the front door as it swings open, banging against the wall behind it. "I am so sorry, Ray-Ray," Ellie's sweet voice rings out and my chest tightens immediately. I set the final plate down on its mat, turning my body toward the door and taking a deep breath. It is now or never.

With my cane gripped tightly, I make my way around the table to see Ellie stop short as her eyes meet mine. "Hello, Sweetheart," I say with a smile, hoping it'll make the reality of the situation slide down easier. Leaning on my cane, trying to support my tired leg, I see the tears well up in her eyes and hope against all hope that they are tears of happiness and not rejection.

~~~~

Ellie

"Hello, Sweetheart," his words ring through my head as I try and comprehend that he's standing here in my cousin's dining room. I wasn't expecting him to be here, I was just coming for dinner, but here he is.

His tall frame, built and toned, with the freckles dotting his handsome face framing his hazel eyes that are working me over, making me blush. No one else says anything as Bobby and I just look at each other, the tears trying to spill over in my eyes as my chest tries to get air into my lungs, heaving in and out.

"Bobby?" is all I can say, my voice squeaky and shaky. I almost feel like turning and running, the tightness in my chest spreading out through my arms and legs and making me feel weak, but I stand my ground.

He gives me a small smirk of a smile and it lightens

the weight on my heart the tiniest bit. Taking a deep breath, I take in as much air as I can, noticing the cane he's leaning on. It confuses me and I move my gaze from the cane to his legs and have to put my hand over my mouth to stop the insulting gasp from escaping.

He lost his leg.

"Oh my God, Bobby," I whisper, seeing the hurt run across his features as he turns and sits in one of the kitchen chairs. I don't know what to say, I just stand there not moving.

Rhea's approaching figure draws my attention from Bobby and she pulls me to the side, out of sight of the kitchen. Her warm hands shake the unease in the surprise presence of Bobby from my body and the tears that had been at bay flow freely down my cheeks. Not for me, but for Bobby.

"Don't do that," she chides in a whisper, her fingers gripping into my arm. Looking into her familiar blue-grey eyes I see her brows knit together. "He's having a hard time. Don't act like this in front of him. He needs you to be a source of strength for him." She repeats the words I remember hearing her tell me once before.

The advice Rosa gave her about Chad's deployment. *Stay strong. Don't waver. Be their pillar of hope.*

"How come you didn't tell me?" I whisper back, defending my reaction as I hear the voices in the kitchen pick up a casual conversation about sports. I would have reacted totally different if I had at least had a warning or a little inkling as to what his injury was. Chad and Rhea hadn't told me anything, so I had no idea that it was as major as him losing his leg, or part of his leg.

"He wanted to tell you," Rhea sighs, leaning her head on my shoulder and hugging me tight to her. "Just let him talk when he's ready, okay Ell?"

There are so many questions floating through my head right now that I want to ask him. How? When? Where? Can I just leave it alone and let him tell me when he's ready?

Taking in a deep breath I let it out slowly, knowing that I can. "Okay Rhea," I whisper, hugging her back and kissing her cheek.

Turning back toward the kitchen with her hand in mine, I keep my eyes on the floor; not wanting to catch myself staring at Bobby's leg again and make him nervous or self-conscious. He's facing the others at the table, his back to me, and I slowly make my way over, taking a pitcher of tea from Rosa as she smiles sweetly. I turn toward Chad and Reno, setting the pitcher down in the middle of the table.

Sitting next to Bobby, I have no idea what to say. I can feel his eyes flit to me every so often, but I don't know where to start. I'm afraid I'll say something stupid, putting my foot in my mouth and embarrassing him or myself.

"How have you been, Sweetheart?" His smooth voice finds me as Chad and Reno chat away about spring turkey season and fishing. I turn my face toward him and see his hazel eyes on me; pulling me in and making me feel as if we're the only ones here.

It's strange how he has such an effect on me, but I like it. With his elbows on the edge of the table and his chin rested in his hands, he's gazing at me as if I'm something important and everyone else can just disappear and he'd be okay with that.

"I've been good," I whisper with a smile, feeling the rush of heat over my skin and kicking myself for the girlish reaction to his attention. "I've missed you," I say all of a sudden, shocking myself and my eyes go wide seeing Bobby's do the same, his eyebrow raising and a smirk coming to those sexy lips. I just opened a can of worms and I can't help but giggle to myself.

He doesn't bring it up all throughout dinner as we all talk over other topics, laughing and joking as the two babies coo and make a mess of themselves with their applesauce. Saying goodnight to Reno and Rosa along with Marisol, Chad and Rhea disappear upstairs to bathe Charlie and put him to bed, giving Bobby and me a stolen moment alone. Turning out of the bathroom, I see him standing at the sliding door looking out on the back yard and seeming sad with his cane propped up against the glass.

It breaks my heart seeing the solemn look on his face, a face that normally would be smiling and laughing. I can hear him sigh heavily as I approach, his hurt filtering through me and bringing my hidden pains to the surface.

*'You're a baby killer. You're a whore'.* Jake's voice breaks through, making me remember who I never want to be again. My hands clench together out of anger at myself for thinking about Jake at a time like this. Trying to shake it off, I take in Bobby's figure once more trying to sort out what I'm about to say.

"I have scars, too, Bobby," I whisper as he turns around slowly and I step up to only be a breath away from him. Tears are threatening to leak out again as I look up at those handsome hazel eyes that are so full of pain. His chest is heaving and I can almost feel the turmoil rolling off of him. I can only think I know how he feels until he talks to me about it, but I can bet he feels incomplete. Almost as if he's broken in body and soul. Lightly putting my hands on his chest, I feel his muscles tense under his t-shirt.

"I don't want to hold you back, Ellie," he mumbles, still not meeting my gaze. He's looking everywhere but at me so I take a step into him, being careful not to bump his leg. "I'm not the same man that I once was."

"I would never expect you to be," I almost sob, my pent up feelings for this man boiling to the surface as his presence sinks in and he finally looks at me, a crease forming in his brow.

Reaching up, I run my fingers tenderly over his eyebrows, trying to soothe the worry. I run my hand up his chest, stopping to rub my thumb along his jaw and resting my fingers at the back of his neck; gently massaging the spot I know he likes. I relax when I feel his arm snake around my waist, pulling me to him. "The way you make me feel hasn't changed. I still want to see you."

"Are you sure?" he whispers against my hair, resting his chin on my head as I breathe him in, feeling safe as his familiar scent surrounds me. It is strange how just the scent of his cologne can make me feel so much better, but it does and I rest my nose on his chest loving the warmth that comes off of him.

"I'm sure." I smile into his shirt, wrapping my other arm around his neck as I go up on my tip-toes. "Now just hold me," I beg with my lips against his cheek. I can't help but let a few tears slip out as he pulls me in tighter, wrapping both arms around my waist.

I can't tell you how long we stood there, wrapped

up in each other while saying nothing. I'm just listening to his breathing and the sound of his lips as he kisses my hair and forehead every now and then.

His arms tighten around my waist, lifting me off the floor and I squeal. "What are you doin'?"

"Carrying you off to cuddle with me." He grins as I angle my head back to see his face.

I almost protest that he shouldn't be carrying me, but as he takes us the short distance into the spare bedroom, I keep my mouth shut letting him set me on the edge of the bed. I watch him as he quietly shuts the door. Turning back to me with a sly smile, he leans his cane against the bedside table and plops down on the bed, throwing his hands behind his head and propping himself up.

I give him a skeptical look and he throws his arms up. "Just cuddling," he makes an X motion over his heart, "I swear."

With a roll of my eyes I sigh dramatically, joining in as he laughs. Kicking off my worn out Converse, I scoot back, leaning against the headboard next to him. I try not to look at his leg, but I can't help it and I can see him watching me.

"You wanna know how it happened?" he asks.

"Only if you wanna tell me," I say honestly, not wanting him to feel as if I'm pushing him to tell me. Leaning my head on his shoulder, I smile as his arm snakes behind my neck pulling me in closer as he sighs. As he starts to talk quietly my hand rests on his abdomen, twirling into the material and twisting it back and forth.

Listening to the story of his injury, I sink further into his chest and his embrace, eventually slinging my leg over his waist as we both sink down onto the pillows. It feels good to be in his arms and as he talks away, I can't help but let some tears fall.

He is a hero, saving Uclid and those Marines from injury, and I don't think he realizes it. I try not to let him see that I'm crying, but the tears drip down onto his shirt and I can feel his arm tighten around me.

He yawns loudly and I giggle, leaning my chin on his chest and smiling at him. "You want me to get goin'?" His reaction makes me laugh even harder as he snaps his chin down, giving me the most ridiculous look as if I'm crazy or that I have three heads.

"No way, Sweetheart." He smiles, pulling me in even tighter. "You're not going anywhere." I sigh and settle into his chest, hearing him mumble in agreement.

I'm glad Bobby shocked me with his presence tonight. He is finally here and he is holding me. He's on his way to being healthy. It feels like everything might be okay for once. It's a nice feeling.

# CHAPTER 7

## BOBBY

*May 1, 2013*

The air is hot and thick around me as I shift and adjust my flack, keeping my eye through the scope of my rifle, focused on the building in front of my position. I can see my team mates glowing in green as they creep silently around the corner of the building in a tight snake pattern, their hands on one another's shoulders.

"Timmons," French's voice comes over the radio and I acknowledge him with an 'all clear'.

I can see him wave Black, Benson, Talbot, and the others into the building and I focus back in on the top row of windows just waiting for movement to catch my eye. Elliot Uclid shifts slightly beside me in his normal spotter position and I spare him a split second look.

"What's your issue?" I whisper, watching as my teammate's lights ascend the stairs within the building and they chatter over the radio saying how all the rooms are empty so far. Maybe this mission is a dud. Faulty intelligence and timing could have screwed us over on this one, leaving us out here in the sweltering desert for nothing.

"I'm still chafed at being yelled at 'cuz of your dumb ass," Elliot retorts in a harsh whisper. Ah, so this is why he's been silent instead of his yammering self. Just because the LT sat us down a couple of days ago and reamed us out because of our low range score and crappy performance on training in the last couple of weeks.

It is mostly my fault in bringing Uclid down with me. I have been lost in day dreams about Ellie and being back in the States taking her on dates and long walks. Yes; I was dreaming of going on walks with her, but hell, who wouldn't with a little hottie like her? She is gorgeous in every way. Funny, smart, and great to be around. Just the thought of her laugh makes a smile break out across my face.

"SEE," Uclid snaps, elbowing me in the shoulder lightly and bringing me back to reality. "You're doing it right fucking now." He's right, and shaking my head to try and clear my thoughts, I focus my eyes back on the building and the lights still ascending floor by floor.

Giving him a grumble of a reply, my nerves go on full alert when a bright flash of light and loud crack fill the silent night air, originating from the building we are watching. My breath catches in my chest and both Elliot and I are up on our feet, racing down the flights of stairs keeping our guns up at the ready. Calling for French, Black, or anybody I'm frantically yelling into the radio, requesting a QRT, or Quick Response Team, to respond to our location. As Elliot and I enter the still smoke filled building I finally breathe as I hear Black's familiar voice come through loud and clear.

"We're all okay," he says and I'm more than rejoiced. I wouldn't be able to deal if my team had gone down while I was day dreaming. This is why I can't do it. I have to get a grip. Climbing the stairs with Uclid watching my six, I'm just kicking myself. I can see their rifle mounted flashlights flickering around the room as I round the corner and I am happy to see them all on their feet.

"What the fuck happened?" French yells, obviously suffering from temporary hearing loss due to the loud explosion. They are all covered in thick dust and I can tell they are trying to regain their bearings. Moving past Benson on the point, I move up into the next stairwell checking for insurgents.

A loud yell from my best friend, my spotter, Elliot Uclid, stops me in my tracks; mixing with the sound of something bouncing down the stairs. Something that is metallic to be exact.

Isn't it funny how some sounds or smells you never forget? Like the smell of freshly mowed hay, or wet earth after a rain. But no, this is a sound I wish I had never heard and hope to never hear again. Looking down at my feet, I see the round orb sitting content between my boots, seemingly staring up at me and laughing.

The bright explosion and heat fill the air around me and it seems to fill my very soul as I take a sharp breath in, shocking myself awake with my eyes locked on the ceiling fan of the spare bedroom in Chad and Rhea's home. I'm drenched in sweat, breathing heavily. As I shift I feel a weight resting on my left arm. Snatching my arm out from under it quickly while wrapping my other arm over it to defend myself I have to stifle a gasp as I see Ellie's petite figure replacing that of what I thought was an enemy.

Her short dark hair is falling across the pillow and her lashes are fluttering ever so slightly against her cheeks as I stay my movements, hoping against all hope that she'll stay asleep and not be awoken by my rash fear filled action. Oh God, if I hadn't recognized her and hurt her in anyway...I don't know what I'd do with myself.

Sitting up, tight pains shoot up through my left leg causing me to grit my teeth silently as I'm keeping my eyes on Ellie's sleeping form. She shifts, mumbling something as I take my arm from around her waist and slide slowly out from under the sheets. I make a beeline for the door, leaving my cane behind.

I don't need the God damn cane. I want to feel the pain and make my awake state real in my mind, because I don't want to relive the nightmare.

The living room is dark and silent as I wobble my way to the large window and pull back the curtains to stare up at the full moon. I can't seem to get my breathing under control, and as the rage and fear rip through my every fiber, my teeth grind together along with my fists clenching and unclenching in rapid succession. I don't want to feel like this, like the whole world is crushing down on me and I reach for my sweatshirt resting on the back of the couch, pulling the front door open as gentle as I can.

The cool spring air nips at my bare skin as I break from the house, walking hurriedly down the sidewalk past Reno and Rosa's. I ignore the pain as it radiates throughout my lower body. If I ignore it, maybe it will go away. If I ignore it, maybe I'll wake up from *this* nightmare and have my life back. I'll wake up to my right life, my SEAL life, the one that Ellie would be happy to share with me. My walk turns into a jog and as the pain shoots up from my mangled left leg, I grit through it and keep going faster.

This pain and heaviness in my chest is squeezing so hard that I can't hold in a frustrated scream, giving in to the pain and falling to the gravel. This reality is bullshit. What the hell did I ever do to deserve this?

I served my country. I did what was asked of me. I saved the helpless and took down potential threats to my nation's freedom. And now what do I have? I have half of my left leg and nightmares. I've given more than just a piece of me, I've given my soul and I can't help but feel right now that I want it back.

"No," I yell at myself, slamming my clenched fists down onto the gravel feeling it bite into my skin but I'm not letting it phase me. "I can't be like this. I need to pick myself up. There are those that I care about that need me."

I repeat the words my psychologist has given me to say in moments of doubt, mumbling them to myself as I push back up onto my feet and straighten the sneaker on my prosthetic. The pain and heaviness in my chest still pulls away at my heart as I turn back toward my temporary home, kicking the gravel under my feet as I chat to myself.

"I will always be a SEAL," I get out between clenched teeth as I grind them back and forth, focusing in on the sound and feel rather than the fire building in my left knee. "I will always be the man that became the sailor." Chad had repeated something similar to me while I was still in the hospital and it has stuck with me ever since. It's hard to believe right now, but as I make it across their driveway as silently as I can, I keep running the words through my mind, wanting to make them true.

Shutting the door behind me without a sound, I pause and listen to see if there is any movement in the house. Nothing but silence meets my ears and I release a quiet sigh of relief. No one noticed my freak out. It's a good thing, because now I won't have to explain it.

Peeking in around the door to my new bedroom I can see the sheets still tangled around Ellie and hear her quiet rhythmic breathing. It brings a sly smile to my face, and for a split second I forget about the pain.

"You better put some ice on your leg, Timmons," Chad's familiar voice fills the dark space and I whip around to see him leaning against the wall separating the kitchen and the living room, a glass of water in his hand. His eyebrow is raised as I see his gaze move from my face to my leg, causing a squirming feeling to race over my skin as his Chief and superior attitude makes me feel like a newbie again. The respect and gratitude that I have for my friend will always remain strong, no matter what I go through.

"I didn't think anyone was up, Chief," I whisper, moving away from the bedroom door and trying not to limp too much as I make my way past Chad to the table, lowering myself down into one of the wooden chairs. The thick pad feels heavenly on my burning and tweaking muscles and I let out a little sigh as Chad joins me still, giving me a skeptical look.

"I woke up when I heard the door to my home open and close in the wee hours of the morning." His fingers tap along the glass and I kick myself, knowing that he would have heard me if I wasn't clouded by pain and panic. The man hears everything. How could I have been so careless as to think that he would let this slide?

"Talk to me, Bobby. I'm your friend, and I'm here to help."

Rubbing my hand across my chin, I nod my head letting my friend know that I acknowledge he's here for me. The pain running up through my leg pulls at my attention. Pushing my chair back from the table I pull the metal prosthetic off and tug on the suspension sleeve, feeling relief as the cool air meets the irritated skin when it's off. It's the first time I've really let anyone have a good look at my leg without the sleeve on and I can just feel Chad's gaze skirt over my knee, but I can't blame him. He has to know what he's up against as my friend, am I right?

Leaving the sleeve off, I pull myself back to the table and run my hand across my face, trying to prepare my mind for the words that I'm going to say out loud. "I'm having nightmares, Chief," I say with my face downturned and my fingers picking at something invisible on the hardwood tabletop.

I feel as if I'm breaking some un-written rule talking about something as childish as having nightmares with the man who basically molded me into the SEAL and man that I am. He taught me and guided me, watching my six and taking me down a few pegs when I needed it.

He nods, adding, "I guessed as much," as he gets up and walks over to the sink, filling a glass from the tap and bringing it back to slide it in front of me while taking his seat once more. I take a sip and sit in silence, letting the faint sunlight from the nearing sunrise pull my attention.

"I don't think she realizes how much this will change things," I mumble, looking back to Chad and seeing his gaze on the pending sunrise as well. His chair is balancing on the two back legs as he leans back, bringing the glass up to his lips as he nods.

I just can't get rid of the feeling that I shouldn't try and tie Ellie down with being with a cripple like me. Taking a deep breath I turn my eyes to the empty and still darkened living room, adding, "I can't be the man that she needs."

"Why don't you let Ellie decide that for herself?" he says, giving me a matter-of-fact look as he slides his chair back again, rising to put his glass in the sink. I watch him as he fills and turns on the coffee pot, pulling a pan of prepared cinnamon rolls from the fridge and placing them on the stove top as he turns the oven on. All that I can think of is that I honestly don't know if I can handle the rejection that might come with letting Ellie in and then having her turn me away.

"Ellie is stronger than you give her credit for." He gives me a wink as he leans back against the counter. Shaking my head, I lean back, rubbing my hand along what's left of my shin and trying to release some of the tension. A good hot shower will do me good, releasing the pains in my leg and in other places.

"Just don't break her heart." He gives me a stern look but can't hold onto it and breaks out in a smile.

"If you break her heart, I'll be the one to suffer."

Laughing, I reach for my crutches that are lying across the opposite chair, taking my metal prosthetic and sleeve in my grip as I prop myself up. "Don't worry, Chief," I smile, giving him a sarcastic wink that I know he'll rag on me for later, "I'm done with my heart breaking days."

As I make my way into the hallway bathroom I hear his hearty laugh, making me smile as I shut the door. If Ellie gives me a chance, I truly will be done with my heart breaking days.

Only time will tell. And as far as I'm concerned, I'll give Ellie all the time she wants as long as I get to spend it by her side.

~~~~

*Ellie*

I can hear Chad and Bobby talking quietly out in the kitchen, trying hard not to let their voices travel. They are talking about me and at first it makes me smile and my heart skip a beat, but then Chad says something like "*She's stronger than you give her credit for*" and it makes me hold my breath, pulling the sheet up around my chin.

Am I strong enough? Am I strong enough to be the support that I know Bobby will need? Better yet, am I strong enough to even start another relationship right now? I don't know if I am.

Yes, the feelings I have for Bobby have only tripled since his deployment and having him just cuddle with me tonight made me feel safe and loved, but am I ready to take it up a notch?

I would feel a hell of a lot better about it if I had those divorce papers signed and in my possession, but as always Jake is taking his sweet time while making my life hell. I am thankful that he hasn't been bothering me lately, but I know he probably isn't far off. He isn't one to give up on something.

I can smell the coffee brewing and the faint hint of cinnamon in the air from Rhea's famous cinnamon buns. I take a deep breath in, savoring the feeling of being home. I love staying in my cousin's house.

Chad is humming to himself as he shuffles past the slightly open door and I hear him go up the stairs. Slowly sitting up, I stretch up to the ceiling, wishing Bobby was in here so we could cuddle some more. Just the thought of his arm wrapped around me makes a little smile caress my face as I reach for my sweatshirt.

"What are ya smilin' at, Sweetheart?" His strong smooth voice scares me and I jump back from the edge of the bed, far enough to hit my head on the headboard. The sharp little pain radiates through the back of my head and I close my eyes, letting a few curses slip out.

The bed dips on my left and I feel Bobby's arms gently snake around me, one at my waist as the other hand covers mine where I bumped my head. Just the slightest touch makes my pulse race.

"I didn't mean to scare ya." He chuckles as I open my eyes, now slightly teary from the ridiculousness of the situation. His hazel eyes are peering down at me, pulling me in, and I can't help but laugh. He's shirtless and glistening, probably from the shower, and as I continue to laugh, he smiles right along with me, wrapping me in a tight hug and toppling us over to lie side by side on the bed.

"No really," Bobby gets out between laughing and running his hand gently over my hair, "are you okay, Ell?"

As I try and control myself, wiping the tears from laughing so hard from my cheeks, I really look into Bobby's eyes. He is staring right back at me, the mixture of green and brown in his eyes being a perfect combination. The freckles across his nose and cheeks make him look so boyish, and as I hesitantly lay my hand over them, he leans into my touch and smiles a heartbreaking smile. It takes my breath away and the slight stubble on his cheek brings the nerve endings in my palm to life.

"I'm okay Bobby," I say but it comes out in a breathy whisper as his look doesn't waver, his attention making a hot blush quickly flow across my skin. The heat rising to the surface matches the feeling in my core, wanting him and needing him, but feeling unsure at the same time.

"That's good," he whispers as I see his look wash over my face. His fingers come up to lightly trace my chin and it sends lightning bolts over my skin, causing goose-bumps to pop up.

"Are you cold?" he asks, shifting closer to me while wrapping his arm around my torso pulling me closer to him.

"No," I barely get out as his hand caresses my cheek again. I've never felt like this, so broken down and so helpless at a touch. I feel as if my body is worthless, my arms refusing to move when I try and wrap them around his neck. A smart ass smile quirks up one side of his mouth.

"So, you're sayin' I'm doing this to you?" he almost laughs out, pulling me slowly to him so that our noses are touching.

I can't answer him. My chest is heaving in and out from just the thought of what might come next. My eyes are trained on his chin, afraid to meet his because then I know I'll be a goner.

Finally, my arms respond enough so that I rest my palms on his bare chest, feeling the warmth and slight moisture from his shower and a flash of what he might look like naked flows through my mind, forcing me to shut my eyes and bite my lip. This man must have a drug in his blood to have me all tangled like this.

"Ellie, look at me," he whispers, his minty breath washes over my face as his fingers gently force my chin up, my eyes meeting his as my nose brushes against his cheek. It seems as if we sit there for hours, just staring at each other, but before I know it Bobby's lips are on mine as his fingers trace a path along my chin and tangle into my hair, encircling the base of my neck.

It's like nothing I've ever felt before as his lips move over mine and my eyes slide shut to savor the moment. Just as I feel his tongue trace a light path over my lips, he breaks away, resting his forehead on mine. I miss the contact immediately, wanting more and feeling as if I *need* more. My heart is pounding so that it's playing a rapid beat in my ears and I can feel a slight tremble tingling in my fingers.

"Ellie, I…" he starts to say, but I quiet him with slamming my lips down onto his. I don't know what has come over me, but I just feel as if I need him more than I need anything right now. I need this man to kiss me; I need his hands on me. I can tell he's shocked at first, but as I nip at his bottom lip slightly he groans, opening for me as I push him onto his back and straddle him. I run my hands slowly and teasingly up his chest, barely tracing his skin with my fingertips.

Now I don't really think about it, but as his hands slide down my sides to rest on my butt, I remember I'm only in skimpy little sleep shorts that I leave here in case I sleep over and a tank top, but I don't care. His fingers grip into my flesh, boosting me up and pulling me tighter to him at the same time as I deepen the kiss while tangling our tongues. It's an amazing feeling as he knows just what I like and matches every move of my lips with his.

As I press myself into his chest, I can feel his rising desire pressing against the basketball shorts he has on and it makes my heart beat faster. He's feeling what I'm feeling. He squeezes my butt cheeks in his hands and I let out a moan against his lips, losing myself in his movements.

"*Ahem*," the shrill, obnoxious throat clearing seems to echo through our little world and we are startled apart.

I turn my head toward the door to see Rhea standing there, Charlie on her hip, with her hand trying to cover the infant's eyes as he pulls at it. I can feel the flush run over my skin as she clears her throat one more time. Charlie coos and gurgles when he sees me, fighting like hell to have his mother let him down so he can crawl and explore the room.

"Sorry to interrupt," she says, and I can tell she's trying not to blush or laugh. "But I was wondering if you two were gonna come eat somethin'?"

"We'll be right out, Rhea." Bobby chuckles, wrapping his arms around my torso tight as Rhea shuts the door behind her. I can just imagine what she's going to go whisper to her husband the second she gets into the kitchen, so turning my face into Bobby's shoulder I can't help but giggle. I don't know what came over me just now, but it felt damn good.

Next thing I know, I'm on my back with Bobby hovering over me, his elbows resting on either side of my face, effectively pinning me down with my legs still wrapped around his waist. I can feel him playing with my hair as his eyes lock onto mine, that evil little grin creeping up once more.

"Don't think I'm done with you, Miss Ellie," he whispers only a split second before claiming my lips with his, pulling my face closer to his with his hands on my cheeks.

His tongue darts over my lips and I open for him, letting him explore as our tongues mingle. It's perfect, the feeling of him kissing me and his weight on top of me. I've never felt this surge of desire before, and as I push my hips up into him, feeling that he's still as ready as before, he moans into our kiss pulling at my hair lightly.

"I'm far from done with you," he adds in a quick break, kissing me a few more times before grumbling that he has to get dressed. As he rolls over to get something out of the dresser on the other side of the room, I immediately miss his weight on top of me. My heart is still soaring, feeling as if it might beat right out of my chest as I sit up, stunned from our feverish display.

I'm on cloud nine while pulling on some jeans and watching Bobby's perfect physique do the same out of the corner of my eye. He adjusts his prosthetic before pulling the jean leg down over it and I can't help but wonder if he's hurting right now. Here I am on cloud freaking nine, not thinking about anything, and he could be in pain. Pulling on a graphic tee and tying my hair up, I bounce across the bed to sit next to him.

"Are you in pain?" I whisper, leaning my head on his shoulder as he buttons up a pearl snap shirt.

"No, not really," he shrugs, throwing his arm around my waist and lifting me off the bed as he stands. Setting me down, he pulls me flush to his front, coaxing me up on my tiptoes with his fingers under my chin so he can place a sweet kiss on my lips. "The only pain I have is in my pants, Sweetheart."

"Oh," I say, blushing wildly as he laughs. He grabs my hips, pulling me in so tight that his erection grinds against my stomach through our clothes and it sets my body on fire. He smiles, seeing the red fill my skin again and kisses me quickly, releasing me and swatting me in the butt.

He follows me out into the kitchen and we join Rhea and Chad for breakfast. Thankfully, neither of them bring up what Rhea interrupted, and as Chad and Bobby head out into the garage to work on Chad's truck, or just talk about us, Rhea lets out a loud dramatic sigh at her position next to me at the sink.

"Go on," I say, elbowing her slightly, "say what you got on your mind."

"It was quite a scene I walked in on." She smiles wickedly, plunging her hands into the soapy water to scrub another glass.

"We were just kissing," I defend myself; trying not to drop the plate I'm drying when the memory of Bobby's lips on mine flows through my mind. The lingering desire lies within and I have to place my hands on the counter to steady myself as my limbs feel weak.

"Yeah. Kissing." She laughs, practically throwing a couple of the glasses back into the water as she almost doubles over in laughter. That's my cousin for ya, always one to not miss a thing.

As I stand there patiently, waiting for her laughing spell to wane, I smile right along with her. It does feel good, knowing he wants me as bad as I want him. But am I ready to take that leap?

"Just listen, Ellie," Rhea's voice breaks my thinking as her arm snakes around my waist. I throw my arm over her shoulder and we stand there for a minute, just two cousins enjoying one another's presence. "Give each other time. You're both still kind of fragile. I just don't want either of you to get hurt. Especially not you."

Turning my cousin around, I hug her fully, wrapping my arms around her shoulders and holding her tight as she does the same around my waist. Rhea is a beacon of strength for me. Surviving the love of her life being deployed, then being shot three times herself, she is one of, if not the strongest person I know. She is a great friend, an awesome wife, and an even better mother. I can only hope to be like her if I get the chance at a family.

"Oh Rhea," I whisper, kissing her on the cheek and releasing her, returning to our small pile of dirty dishes. "Please don't worry over me." She huffs and I know that won't stop her from worrying day and night, but I can try to ease her mind when I can.

Hearing Bobby's laugh float in from the garage, I smile, letting the sound of it wash over me. Can I do this? Can I be the woman he needs me to be? Will he want me after all my secrets are revealed?

I can only take one day at a time and hope that after it all, I can be the one for him and he can forgive my mistakes.

# CHAPTER 8

*Ellie*

*May 11, 2013*

I was having such a great dream about Bobby and

me that I don't want to get out of bed right now, but my morning run is calling my name. So without lack of groaning, I pull myself from the cheap little twin bed and pull on some shorts and a tank, not caring how my hair looks as I pull the short locks into a ponytail.

Since Bobby has moved in with Rhea and Chad, we've seen each other almost every day. We've gone on walks to the back of their property, sneaking away like teenagers to make out in the tall grass, fooling around, but we haven't had sex yet. Not that we haven't wanted to, but we've decided to wait until the time seems right. We still want to get to know each other as much as possible.

Which is nice because there is just something about Bobby that makes me want to wait. I want it to be more than just two horny people getting it on. I want it to be about us, and I want it to be significant enough and at the point in time when I know I'm strong enough to be what Bobby needs. When I know I can be strong enough to support him in the life he will be leading.

I don't know what it is but that boy makes me feel like a school girl again. Even now, as I'm tying my sneakers I can't help but smile and laugh quietly at the thought of us playing twenty questions while sitting out by Rhea's fire-pit. We had gone over first loves, favorite music, favorite foods, favorite places to be, and had found out we have a lot more in common than we first thought. We both love country and rock music, along with loving hamburgers piled high with pickles and onions, and being on a farm. He had thrown his arm around me and pulled me onto his lap, whispering in my ear that we might be made for each other. The smile on my face widens as his smooth voice plays over and over in my head while I put my ear-buds in, cranking up my iPod with some Luke Bryan.

Heading out of my trailer park, I wave at Melody and Jude, sitting on Jude's makeshift patio as they drink their morning coffee. I haven't been as close with Melody lately as before our little incident at the Virginia Beach club, but I'm still cordial to her. No reason to be overly nasty.

I turn toward the edge of town. I haven't run this way in a while and today seems like the perfect day to venture toward my old town of Waverly. Maybe I'll even stop in at the Spring's family farm and see my old friend Lady.

The gravel crunches under my feet as I keep a steady pace, hovering at the stop signs and intersections long enough to make sure nothing is coming and admiring the springtime warmth from the sun. Small daisies and tulips are starting to pop up on the side of the road as I near the town line, humming away to Volbeat as they drum onto my playlist.

Horns honk and I wave at the smiling faces that pass me slowly on the road, taking extra care to wave to the Wakefield sheriff and his deputy when they flash their lights at me as I jog by their speed trap hideout. They both tip their coffee cups to me as I smile, singing lowly to myself.

As I round a slight corner, nearing the Springtime Equine Farm, I immediately know there's something wrong. There are horse trailers parked all along their driveway and a few along the road; more than they own. There aren't any horses in the pastures and on a nice day like this, that is a red alert in my mind. I pick up my pace and by the time my feet hit the loose gravel of their driveway I'm sprinting, my breathing heavy and fast.

The youngest son, Bryan Spring, is the first I see and I wave at him, ripping the ear-buds out as I skid to a stop. I can see the sadness plain across the young boy's face and as he gets closer, I notice the slight tears building on his lashes.

"What's goin' on?" I ask between heavy breaths, trying to relax before I overload on nerves and exertion. The boy turns his face up to me just as a few tears slip out from his big brown eyes. My heart starts to break, even not knowing the situation.

I had waved and talked to this boy almost every day while I lived in the Waverly trailer park, stopping and helping him feed the horses when his father was away getting groceries and supplies. I have watched him grow at least six inches in height and even now his pants don't fit him quite correctly, being more high water skimmers than regular jeans. Now, seeing him torn up over something I can't help but let it affect me, the tightness in my chest from running turning into nervousness and a little fear.

"We gotta sell the horses," he sniffles, scraping the back of his dust covered hand across his face, smearing the tears and dirt in a path across his cheek.

"What?" I say, baffled. Huge equine farms like theirs usually do great in small towns like this and they are selling their form of profit? There must be something wrong. Just as I'm about to ask him what happened, I hear gruff voices coming from the barn followed by a string of distressing whinnies. With my mouth agape I follow Bryan's stare as his gaze flits over to the barn.

His father, Kelley, is helping two men load three horses into a trailer and one of them is Lady. Before I realize what I'm doing, I'm sprinting to them, sloshing through mud puddles from last night's rain and hopping over stray piles of manure. Sliding around the edge of the trailer I catch the reins of Lady's lead, yanking them from the scruffy man's hands.

"What are you doin'?" I almost scream, looking from the two strangers to Kelley Spring, watching him hand off his horse and scrape his hand back through his blonde hair. He looks worn down, and as he makes his way toward me a wave of disappointment flows over me.

"Miss Ellie, how are you?" he whispers, wrapping his hand around my arm, trying to pull me free from Lady, but I'm not letting go. She's too good of a horse to let these two shady men make off with her and I'm standing my ground.

"What is happening here, Kell?" I plead, tugging for Lady to come to me and she obliges. Her champagne coat is dirty and needs a good brushing as I run my hand over it, patting her lightly as she snorts and bumps her nose into my shoulder. She remembers me. Her eyes tell me she's afraid and that she needs me.

"We need the money somethin' awful," he says, turning his eyes to the dirt and spitting off to the side. He's a country boy through and through and it must be killing him to do this. "I've sold off all the horses, and these men are here to pick up theirs."

"All of them?" I can't believe it. Their family has operated this farm for over sixty years, raising and training some of the best show horses and work horses in all of Virginia. This can't be right.

"All of 'em." He nods, spitting again and giving me a sad look. Out of the corner of my eye I spot his wife in the bay window of the home with a baby on her hip. She waves and I wave back, trying to give her a smile but I know it's strained. Now I know why this is happening.

"Now if you would," Kelley tugs on the reins in my hand, but I don't hand them over, "these men would like to get a move on."

"Not with Lady they aren't," I protest, shaking my head at him and the now laughing men. The Spring family should be able to keep her. She is their best show and work horse after all. She is beautiful and majestic and should be a beacon of hope. She doesn't deserve to be handed off to these two questionable men to go only God knows where to probably be mistreated.

"Ellie, they already paid in cash," Kelley pleads, tugging on the reins and ripping them from my grip as I try to scramble them back. Turning his back on me he starts to lead her into the trailer and my heart is breaking. I can't let this gentle creature go. She's been a symbol of hope for me since the beginning of this journey of mine and I can't let her disappear now.

"I'll double whatever they paid," I yell, getting Kelley to stop in his tracks with his back still to me. The two men are looking at me with open mouths and wide eyes. One cracks up laughing as the silence hangs over us as the other just scratches his beard.

"Ellie you don't have three grand to give me and even if you did," Kelley says, turning his face only slightly to look at me over his shoulder.

"I'll get you the money," I plead, feeling the hurt

in my chest spread, starting to bring tears to my eyes. I fumble with the zipper pocket of my track jacket, almost dropping my cell phone as I pull it out and call Bobby. He's the only one that I can think of at this point that can help me. Plus he's around Chad, who I know will help.

I need them to come help me convince this good hearted man to keep this horse. They can certainly talk some sense into him, can't they?

"Ellie." Kelley turns and looks me full in the face while handing Lady's reins to one of the guys. I'm cursing to myself as to why Bobby isn't answering as the beaten down farmer walks up to me, placing his hands on my shoulders.

"They've already paid," he whispers, patting one of my arms as a few tears slip out onto my cheeks. Hearing Bobby's voicemail I press end and shove my phone back in my pocket, letting the anger I feel for Lady spill out. "I can't afford to give them their money back."

"But," is all I can get out, my voice clipped by the sound of the shutting door to the trailer. My first symbol of hope in my new life is being shipped off, away from the loving family that took care of her and raised her since birth.

I watch as the guys shake hands with Kelley, accepting his apology on my behalf because I can really care less whether or not they are offended. I watch, my heart still in dismay, as the black cloud of exhaust rises up from their diesel stacks. Their tailgate disappears around the slight corner in the direction that I came from, with Lady and two of her companions tucked away in the back, and my shoulders slump.

I feel deflated. My chest hurts with all the tears I'm holding in at seeing my equine friend sold off, and as I look over at little Bryan, I'm pained by the tears he's silently shedding. I can tell he's trying to be a 'man', trying not to let the loss of something as tangible as a horse affect him but it is, I can tell. He was attached to every last one of the horses and it was evident in all the time I would catch him lying in the pasture with them, just staring up at the sky.

"Oh Bry," I whisper, taking him in a one arm hug as his father returns to helping the other buyers with their new horses, loading them and brushing them down. The boy wraps his arms around my waist and rests his cheek on my chest, sobbing as silently as he can. I wish I could be doing the same, but I can't. Not here at least.

I hug Bryan to my chest until the last horse is gone, letting him cry so that his father can help load up the last of his families prized horses and wave at the driver as the trailer disappeared. Kelley comes over and tells his son to go in the house and with one last, tight hug, the boy tells me goodbye, leaving me to deal with the hurt in my own heart for the situation.

"I know it's gonna be hard on the boy," Kelley says, kicking at a stone with his worn out steel toes, sending it flying into his perfectly mowed grass. His statement makes me a bit mad, but I nod, fumbling with my iPod and trying not to let the frustration pour over.

"Yeah, I know," is all I say, turning and waving over my shoulder as I slam the ear-buds into place, ignoring the slight pain I cause myself and turning back toward home. I don't take notice of my favorite tulips or the daisies; I just keep my eyes trained on the road and focus in on the music.

It's Volbeat again, telling me that I'm the sinner in the "Sinner is You". It pulls at the fragile state that my normal calming equine friends puts me in and I let a few tears roll over my lashes as I fail to hesitate at the stop signs. I could care less right now if I got hit. Yeah, it sounds stupid that I'm this torn up over a horse that wasn't even mine, but the fact is, she *was* mine.

Lady was the first good thing that I saw when I lived in Waverly. My morning runs where always lit up by her presence and her meeting me at the fence. She listened as I talked to her, cried to her, and told her some of my darkest secrets. She never judged or belittled me. She never said that I was stupid or dumb, or that I was a whore or a slut. She just stood there with her big brown eyes watching me as I would run my fingers through her champagne coat and dark brown mane. She was my first source of hope until I found Rhea, but Lady still meant the world to me. And now she's gone.

My legs are screaming at me, but I don't stop my quickened pace. I need to work all this tension out; before I get back to my trailer, because if I don't I'll collapse like a worthless pile in the shower and cry my eyes out.

I don't know if I'm more upset for little Bryan and the loss of his precious companions, or for me and the loss of my morning distraction during my run. I realize now why sometimes they use horses in therapy with some children, because frankly they are amazing. There is this sense of calm and acceptance that comes with buddying up with this enormously powerful animal and having it rest it's head on your shoulder. But now, all of that is gone for both me and Bryan.

As I round the last slight curve, now within sight of the trailer park, I let out a heavy sigh and try and immerse myself in humming a little Reba. I know I couldn't have given Kelley the money he deserved for Lady, but it was worth a shot for Bryan's sake and for mine. Watching that gate shut on the trailer was like having a piece of me slammed away with those three horses.

Turning into the drive and waving to Jude as he pulls out, I take a deep breath and push back the tears. Maybe seeing Lady being shipped off was a sign. Maybe it's telling me that I need to move on and get over this hump of being scared to love someone again. Maybe I should take this experience and let go of my hesitant self to embrace my future.

Swinging open my front door, I slam it shut and lean back against it, closing my eyes. Ripping my iPod from my arm and tossing it blindly toward the direction of my ratty couch I listen to my ragged breathing. I don't know if I'm totally ready to let go and with that I know that I am weak. I might be too weak for what Bobby needs in a girlfriend.

"No," I tell myself, snapping my eyes open to stare at the fading floral wallpaper of my living room. "I will not go through this again. I will let things unfold as they will." Letting out a loud and long sigh I toss my jacket over the chair and start stripping for a long, hot shower. I need it.

I crank on the water and step in after settling on something with myself. I will let things work out as they will, being myself and try not to let anyone get me down. I know it's easier said than done, but right now that's all I have to offer myself.

~~~~

# Jake

She doesn't see my patrol car as she jogs by and turns into her trailer park drive, but I sure as hell see her. Her red track jacket, skin tight black jogging pants, bright sneakers on her feet, and white ear-buds in her ears. Oh yeah, I definitely see Ellie Mae.

Just like that day back in high school when I first noticed her for real, as more than just another pretty little thing in the crowd. She was wearing her cheerleading practice booty shorts and grey t-shirt, tied in a knot at the back while exposing part of her stomach. It was a hot day and I was doing drills with the football team, pausing only when I caught a glimpse of her. Since that day, I've been hooked and she's been mine.

Hell, she still is mine. At least she should be. Yeah, sure, when we lived in West Virginia I cheated, a lot, but I'm a man. I have needs.

"Can we get goin' now, Man?" my partner, Tom, whines from the passenger seat, tossing his hat onto the dash and pitching his half empty coffee cup out the window into the grass. I just throw my middle finger up at him and keep my eyes on the run down trailer she disappeared into. I'd sit here all day if I could, because I've done it before.

Ever since the night I woke up and found she had taken off, I've been desperate to get her back. She is my wife and she was carrying my child.

*Was.* Just thinking the word makes my fists ball up against the steering wheel. She killed our baby, not caring what I wanted. She only thought of herself. She is a bitch, and I plan on showing her just how she should be treated because of it.

Since that night I've transferred over to the Virginia State Troopers, knowing she would have come to Wakefield in search of her family. Plus, it pays more than the West Virginia Troopers.

I cornered her back in January in a bar, but her loud mouth friends and cousin stepped in and I had to hightail it out of there. Her complaints and claims fall on deaf ears because one of my superiors is my cousin, so he slides everything under the carpet. It is nice being above the law *and* being the law at the same time.

I can't wait to bring her little world crashing down around her like she deserves. She doesn't know that I know her little secret. That little Virginia Beach secret involving those two homos she likes to hang out with. Oh man, I bet her Navy boy is going to love that one; I bet he'll flip shit. The best part is going to be the look on Ellie's face when I break the news to her friends and family.

*"Your cousin, your friend, is not only a stripper and a whore, but she's a baby killer, too."* Oh it'll break her little heart, just like she did mine.

"Come on, Man," he whines again and I chuck my

sunglasses at him, nailing him right between the eyes and he reels back, smacking his head on the closed window, causing me to burst out in laughter.

"You're a fuckin' asshole," he growls, throwing the glasses back at me, which I catch with little effort before they smash against the window. Tom and I have been friends since the academy and we're cut from the same cloth. We were raised in the true Southern way where the man works and the woman cleans, cooks, and takes care of the kids. Tom and his wife have three boys, all younger than four. I wouldn't want another partner, even if they doubled my salary.

He has helped me stake out her trailer park and that nasty club she strips at, taking photos and just watching her when I'm busy. Tom has been an awesome friend.

I'm reluctant to leave my stakeout, but hearing him grumble in his seat some more, I crank the engine to life pulling the cruiser hesitantly to the edge of the road to make sure none of these Wakefield trash crash into me. Little Ellie is lucky all of her neighbors are home right now, or I'd be paying her a nice little visit.

"I'll be back, sweet thang," I whisper and blow a kiss, pushing my aviators into place before spinning and squealing the tires, heading the hell out of here. I'm not giving up that easy on her. My daddy didn't raise no quitter with that belt of his.

She's my wife, even if those papers sitting on my coffee table at home say she doesn't want to be anymore. We said 'till death do us part' and God damn it, I mean it.

When I get my hands on her I'll show her why she

should've never left me in the first place, laying her in a world of hurt she never thought was possible. If she thought I was a 'wife-beater' before she's in for a little treat.

Even her little Navy boyfriend can't keep her safe; I'll make sure of that.

~~~~

# BOBBY

*ONE, TWO, THREE, FOUR.*
*ONE, TWO, THREE, FOUR.*
Chief's rapid counting keeps the sweat flowing as I pound out the flutter kicks to his rhythm. It feels awesome to be working out with him again, even if it is just in his makeshift gym out in the garage. Just being around a fellow SEAL makes it real.

"Now pushups," he yells, flipping over on his stomach right beside me as I match his movement, smiling the entire time. I'm enjoying it because there is little pain in my leg. I've been fitted with three new prosthetics and I'm putting one of them through the wringer right now.

I replaced that normal old metal one with a curved spring leg for running and working out, taking a lot of the impact away from my leg and absorbing it. I also ordered two regular prosthetics, one just a plain black stainless steel and the other, hand painted by a buddy, with the American flag and eagle, because I have to be badass somehow, right?

My therapist says I should be using my cane less and less now, so I'm trying to stick by that. We'll see after this workout how well that plan sticks as I get to my feet to do some squat thrusts. Chief's been doing a lot of his NCIS work from home so it's been nice having him around to talk to and mess around with. You know the usual, normal guy shenanigans.

I've also been getting closer to Ellie with every passing day. We've snuck out of the house like Romeo and Juliet more than once, making our way to the back of the property to roll around in the tall grass. And I swear that girl's lips can stop my heart. She's almost got me tied around her pretty little finger, and right now I wouldn't mind.

I'll admit, I am falling pretty hard for the girl and I take the ridicule and ribbing from Chad and Reno for it every night. They just don't believe that a notorious playboy like me is going to try and settle down with a down to earth girl like Ellie, but right now it seems to be true. We seem to be heading in a great direction and it makes me feel awesome.

In the last week I haven't had one nightmare. No waking up in the middle of the night, drenched in sweat and shaking from the sound of the grenade. No shaking from the fear that stays in my mind long after I'm awakened. I know the pain is still lingering there, but it's nice to not have to fight it right now. I feel somewhat normal. I feel like Bobby again.

"Alright Bobby," Chief pauses, bending over and breathing hard enough to make me laugh at him.

Granted I'm sweating like a pig, but I've been in the hospital, I have a good reason, "I need a water break."

"Okay, ol' man," I say with a smile, getting a sharp look as he chugs a bottle of water. Taking a long drink from mine, I take a look at my phone and see that I missed a call from Ellie about forty-five minutes ago.

"Hey, what would Ellie be doin' up so early?" I ask turning the face of my phone toward the Chief and letting him see that she had called. It's only eight after eight and I know she worked at the bar last night so I would think she'd still be in bed.

"Probably taking her morning run," he breathes out, chucking the crushed and empty bottle into a bin in the corner and throwing his arms up above his head, stretching.

Looking at my screen, I'm not sure if I should call her back or not. Is there something wrong? Should I text her? I can see Chad still watching me out of the corner of my eye as I set the phone down, still staring at it as if it will do a trick.

"If there was somethin' wrong, she woulda called Rhea," he says, patting my shoulder. "Now let's get back to it." He smiles and I can't help but laugh at my former teammate. As he cranks up the radio, currently playing Volbeat's "Cape of our Hero", I look back at my phone once more before taking the pull up bar.

Should I call her back? Maybe Chad is right.

I'm sure Chad is right, she would've called Rhea if something was wrong or she would've called more than once. Yeah, he's right. I fall into the set of pull-ups he's counting off, matching him move for move and also trying to show off. I might have lost part of my leg, but my cocky attitude is firmly intact.

That attitude got me through BUD/S training and earned me my SEAL trident when everyone told me it was a stupid goal, one that I would never achieve because I wasn't the right kind of guy. Well I showed those assholes. I received my Trident on a Friday morning, on a beach in California during morning roll call. The SEALs that were there proceeded to chase me down the beach, even at my best effort to outrun them, and toss me in the Pacific as per tradition. Then, standing soaked and caked with sand, I endured another SEAL tradition; the pounding of the Trident. One by one the SEALs came up to me and slapped my Trident into my chest as hard as they could, piercing my skin just above my heart over and over and it felt good. It felt good, because after that I was part of a bigger family; a badass family.

About an hour later, Chief and I are done with our workout and horsing around as we stumble into the kitchen, tripping over each other as we push and shove. Right off I see Ellie sitting with Rhea at the kitchen table. Her dark hair is still wet and she's looking as cute as ever when she smiles at me.

"Well good mornin', Beautiful." I smile, making my way over to her and giving her a quick kiss on the cheek. She even smells enticing as a fruity scent flows over me, making me want to scoop her up and take her away right here and now.

"Mornin' Bobby." She smiles, laying her hand gently on my cheek as her blue-green eyes run over my sweaty body. I nod to Rhea and she rolls her eyes at me, smiling at what she calls silly flirting between Ellie and me.

"I hope my husband didn't kick your ass too

much, Timmons." She laughs as Chad leans in and kisses her wildly, taking her face in his hands and rubbing his sweaty cheeks on her as she squirms and yells as him.

"Oh, I think your husband is the one who got his ass kicked." I laugh as Ellie and Rhea both complain to Chad about how gross his actions were. I just laugh some more as he gives me a shit eating grin, wiping his shirt across his face and leaning down to kiss her hard one more time.

"Don't talk too much shit, boy," he warns, turning his back to me to fix a cup of coffee. "I might have to put you in your place like I did in Afghanistan."

"Oh, low blow, Chief." I fake a punch to the gut and plop down in the chair next to Ellie, flinging my arm over the back of hers while lightly running my hand over her back, making her shiver slightly.

I love how I affect her. I can give her goose-bumps with the slightest touch or make her blush with the silliest comment. It's like her body is on edge waiting for me to make her tip over.

All the way through breakfast Chief and I recount stories of our missions, well at least parts that we can tell the girls while still keeping our oath of secrecy, no doubt boring the girls and baby Charlie; but they sit and laugh along with us nonetheless. By the time Ellie and Rhea stand to do the dishes, my hand is entwined with hers resting on the side of her leg just underneath the table. It feels right and I give her a squeeze before letting her follow her cousin to the sink.

"Come on, lover boy," Chad laughs, slapping me slightly on the side of the head while grabbing Charlie up and out of his highchair, "you could use a shower.

You smell like shit."

"Why thanks Chief," I say while flipping him off, heading into my bedroom while he disappears up the stairs with his squirming son. Pulling a pair of jeans and a plaid button down from my drawers I fling my towel over my shoulder and head for the bathroom.

Winking at Ellie as she talks away with Rhea, I nod for her to join me and she blushes slightly turning her eyes back to drying the plates and making me laugh behind the shut door. I'm happy that I haven't hurried to have sex with her. I know that sounds strange coming from a man, especially a self-pronounced man whore like me, but it's true. With Ellie things are going to be different.

Chad was right; I do smell like shit so the shower feels great. Drying off, I decided I'm going to try out my new black metal prosthetic and slide it on over the suspension sleeve, testing it out before pulling my jeans on. It feels like there is nothing there; no pain, no sleeve, no hard plastic or metal parts, and it's great.

Letting a cloud of steam out when I open the door, I turn to see Ellie standing by the glass door, a cup of coffee moving slowly to her lips. Her perfect, plump, sin inducing lips, and I immediately feel a need for her. She's like a drug and I don't think I'll ever want to kick it.

"What are ya doin' by your lonesome, pretty girl?" I ask, rubbing my towel through my hair and tossing it down the basement stairs to land on the washer. She doesn't turn to face me, but a heart stopping smile creeps onto her lips as they rest on the rim of the mug.

"Nothin' much. Just thinkin' how nice the pond out back must be right now." Oh man, the combination of her smile and thinking about her in a bathing suit make naughty little thoughts race through my mind and I can't fight the smile from coming to my lips.

"It's gonna get hot real quick today." She grins again, this time turning to face me with the mug covering her lips. She takes a quick sip, but her eyes never leave mine. Does she know what she's doing to me?

"Oh yeah?" is all I can say, trying not to sound too excited, even though I feel like a teenager after his girlfriend offers him a quickie under the bleachers. Is it just me, or is she sending me a signal?

"Yeah," she smiles again, setting the mug down on the island and pulling the sliding glass door open, "ya wanna come with me?"

"Hell yeah." I try not to yell it as I scramble to button my shirt and find my baseball cap. In less than a minute I have my boots and shirt on, even if half the buttons are crooked, and I'm following Ellie's fine little butt out into the back yard. She's got on these little denim shorts, and it is hard not to stare as she leads me out onto the trimmed trail leading out back.

"You remember that horse I was tellin' ya about?" she says over her shoulder while weaving her way over the tire tracks, picking at the tall grass and twirling it between her fingers.

"Lady, right?" I ask, remembering only the snippets she has told me about the horse she liked to stop and see on her runs when she lived in Waverly. She has a soft spot for animals, like her cousin does, and she's said a few times how she'd like to maybe own a few horses one day. That would be fine with me.

"Yeah," she replies, but her tone turns sad and clipped, and as I watch her walk her shoulders sag and her head tilts to watch her feet. She looks somewhat defeated so I take the few strides between us and wrap my arms around her waist, sinking my face into her hair as she gasps in surprise.

She laughs and swats at my arms, telling me I'm crazy and silently I agree with her. I am crazy; crazy about her.

I put a halt to our slow walk and spin her around, pulling her to me and wrapping my arms around her shoulders as she tucks her face into my chest and encases my waist with her tiny pale arms. The feeling of her held tight to me is enough to drive any warm blooded human mad.

"They sold her," she sighs out, turning her face to rest her chin on my chest, looking directly up at me. There are tears on the edges of her lashes and it hurts my heart to see her sad. She shouldn't ever be sad. I run the pad of my thumb just under her lashes and sweep away the moisture as it slowly seeps out, never moving my stare from hers. She sniffles slightly.

"Well, did you get to say goodbye?" I know letting things go is hard, trust me I'm going through it right now, but sometimes when you get to say goodbye to it, it makes it a little easier. I know it would have made losing my parents a little easier at least.

She skirts her eyes to the side as my arms still hold her to me and she sucks her bottom lip in, biting it and looking so damn sexy that I have to restrain myself from pulling her up and covering her mouth with mine. I brush my fingertips along her cheek and push a stray lock of hair from her face, tucking it behind her ear. Her eyes close for a second and I can feel her relax in my arms, the slight action making a smile break out on my face.

"The boy was so broken hearted," she whispers, resting her cheek on my sternum and tightening her grip around my waist. I can just about feel the pain flowing through her; her breathing shallow and quick, fighting the tears that still linger on her lashes. Hugging her tighter still, I lean down and kiss her hair letting my lips linger to let her know I'm here. I feel a few tears hit my forearm as we stand there, but I say nothing; not because I don't have anything to say but because I know she just wants to be held right now.

A light breeze seems to surround us as we stand there in the knee high grass, just holding each other. Her fingers start to move along my forearm and I can see her tracing the lines of my tattoo, her eyes trained on the black and grey pirate ship. I've had it since my first tour of duty in the Middle East.

"Why a pirate ship, Bobby?" she asks, turning her beautifully pale face up to me while wiping the moisture from her cheeks with her fingertips. Her mascara is starting to run, but it doesn't matter to me. She's just as beautiful with it smeared and smudged as she is without it at all.

Taking my eyes off of her for only a second, I look at my tattoo. The shades of black and grey tangled together in an angry high seas scene. The beaten and battered pirate ship with its tattered Jolly Roger flying high, being tossed around by raging waves with the words 'Refuse to Sink' displayed front and center on the bow. It represented a hell of a lot more right now at this point in my life than it had when I had gotten it inked on my skin in Norfolk.

"I know why you have this," she says, pushing up

my right sleeve and running her fingers along the tribal frog design with the number ten woven into it. The frog pays homage to the history of the SEALs and the number ten is my Team. As her fingers run along my warming skin my breathing speeds up, needing to get my heart beating to move the blood alone before I pass out from the excitement.

"The ship is just a reminder to me that when things get rough, there is always a break in the storm or a sunny port to look forward to." Her eyes look into mine as one of her eyebrows rises in question. The look on her face makes me laugh, and I lean down and kiss her lightly on the lips.

"See," I say pointing to the inside of my arm and the only color in the entire tattoo. A peek at a clear blue sky and green grass on land through the raging storm is my pirate ship's savior.

"Hmmm," I can hear her mumble, "I never noticed the color before." Her look moves up my chest and back into my eyes as a sleek smile plays across those pink lips of hers. I lean in ever so slowly, hoping to get a kiss from those delivery devices of pleasure; but her palms on my chest stop me.

"What other surprises do you have?" she questions, giving me a flirty smile chuck full of attitude as she steps back and places her hand on her cocked hip. Oh the dirty things I could say to her right now that would knock that attitude down to blushing in no time, but no, I'll keep those thoughts inside. For now at least.

As a grin starts to play across my face, Ellie surprises me as she turns and runs through the grass in the direction of the pond, giggling the entire way. "Oh don't run from me, little girl," I yell after her as I take off, bounding through the tall grass and brush after her fleeting figure. I run and laugh, feeling no pain or soreness at all in my left leg as my new prosthetic does its job absorbing the shock and weight and my Timberland boots crunch through the fallen branches.

Rounding a curve in the trail I come to a dead stop, spotting something lying in the grass. Bending over I pick up a blue and white flip flop, turning it over like it's something foreign to me. Is this for real? Am I seeing what I think I'm seeing? Is this a skinny dipping walk?

"Come on Bobby," I hear her yell my name and it sends shocks right up through my spine.

Taking the flip flop with me I pause again to pick up its companion and break the tree line, heading for the pond. Inside the darker tree cover the humidity kicks up a level. Tucking her shoes into the pocket of my jeans I start to unbutton my shirt, hearing Ellie still in front of me making her way through the weeds.

Out of the weeds and standing on the bank, I stop and take in the magnificent scene before me. Her shorts and panties are lying on a tree stump off to my left as her bra and tank top hang from a low lying branch.

Oh yeah, this is happening. Her back is to me as she wades waist deep into the pond and I can see the pair of pointe shoes tattooed on her back. She is so pale and dainty looking that I think I might break her in half when I get in the water.

"*No; take it easy, Bobby,*" I whisper to myself, getting the last button undone and throwing my shirt on top of Ellie's clothing. Pulling my boots off, I'm glad my new prosthetic came with a regular foot shape, because I would sink in the soft mud if it didn't, and I toss them off with my pants and boxer briefs, turning to face the pond.

For a split second I think, "*What the hell am I doin' out in the middle of the woods butt-naked?*", but then I see her turn slightly with her arms covering her chest and the blush that runs over her skin answers my question. I'm here to be with her. The water is cool, but it's nice as I make my way in, not taking my eyes from her as she gets a bit deeper and leans down, swimming a few strokes further away from me.

"Are you gonna keep swimming away from me, or are ya gonna come on over?" I say to her as the water comes up over my waist, making my skin goose-bump from the temperature change. She turns back toward me and smiles, disappearing under the water and leaving ripples in her wake.

"Oh, we want to play games?" I think to myself and smile, sinking underneath the water easily with my eyes open. The water is somewhat clear and calm and I can spot her in a split second trying to sneak up behind me. I wait calmly, holding my breath is like a piece of cake since drown proofing in BUD/S, and I turn on her as I feel her near, grabbing her arms and wrapping her tight to my body and bringing us up to the surface before she has the chance to swallow any water.

She's squirming in my grip and playfully swatting at my arms. As I turn her around she's wiping at her face and I get a good glimpse at her body.

God damn. She is more perfect than I could have wished for. The curve from her hips up to her breasts is like it's never ending. She's still laughing as I run my fingers along the curve of her waist just below her ribs and she stops, almost freezing, her eyes looking into mine.

"Bobby?" she whispers, resting her hands on my chest. Her touch seems to send vibrations all along my skin and I move my hands to her back, pulling her closer to me. This girl is going to break me, her finger tracing a small circle on my pec feels as if it is making my entire body tremble and I let out a ragged breath.

"Are you okay, Bobby?" she whispers, her eyes following the path of her finger as it swirls away on my chest, moving from left to right. The water droplets are trickling slowly down her chest and I desperately want to follow them with my lips and tongue.

"Of course I am, Sweetheart." I smile, lifting her chin with my fingers so her now turquoise eyes look into mine. I love the way they can change color with the light, it keeps me guessing. Leaning forward, brushing my lips just lightly along her jaw I whisper right into her ear, "Are *you* okay?"

"Yes," she says, so softly that I can barely catch it even though I'm only inches away from her lips. Kissing her earlobe, I pull her closer to me as her arms wrap around my chest, her hands splaying out on my shoulder blades. Moving my hand to entangle in her hair as my other cradles her lower back, I move my lips from her ear along her jaw toward her mouth, lingering only a whisper above it.

Her eyes are half open with her dark lashes fluttering against her skin as it flushes to a sweet rosy color and she looks like an angel. My angel. As she squirms in my arms, her nails biting into my back, her stomach brushes against my very erect cock, showing my apparent need for her, and she takes a sharp breath in gazing up at me.

"Tell me what you want, Sweetheart." I smile, rubbing my thumb along her bottom lip and her eyes flutter shut for a second, snapping open as her hands weave their way up my torso. She slowly rises up on her tip toes, holding her body tight to mine and brushing her nose along mine.

"I want you, Bobby," she says, looking me right in the eye.

In this second, I'm complete. Forget the war. Forget my leg. Right here, right now I'm absolutely fucking perfect and I don't hold back, crushing my lips to hers and wrapping my arms under her butt while lifting her up and locking her legs around my waist.

~~~~

*Ellie*

"Bobby," I breathe out as our lips part from their frenzy, his moving down my neck with his teeth grazing the crux and sending a ripple of desire through me.

"What is it, Sweetheart?" he murmurs, moving his lips down my chest as I can't help but lean back, letting him explore every inch of me like he never has before. His hands are supporting me with one at my back, splayed across my spine, while the other is scooped under my butt. I squeeze my legs tighter around his waist, not wanting to ever let him go from this moment on.

I feel his very large cock brush against my core and doubts flash through my mind. Should I be doing this? Is this the right time for us?

Yes, this is the right thing. Feeling his fingers flex against my skin, my heart skips and I know this is what I want. I want Bobby.

"Not here," I get out of my fuzzy mind, but what I really want to say is, *"Now, please God, now!"* The way his lips move along mine and across my skin is like nothing I've ever felt before and I need him to be mine in this stolen moment. Forgetting about my past; forgetting about my secrets and faults; forgetting about the world outside this beautiful backwoods paradise for a while with just the two of us as one.

Spinning us around, Bobby starts heading toward the bank as I take his lips with mine, my hands holding the sides of his face. The day old scruff on his cheeks is rough against my touch but I don't mind. I entangle my tongue with his and teasingly bite at his bottom lip, loving the way he grumbles at me and smiles after I release it.

He stumbles and I bring myself back to reality feeling stupid, and looking him right in the eye. "Are you okay Bobby? I mean your leg? Do you need to set me down? I can walk if you need…"

My partly frantic rant is cut off by his lips as he

claims my mouth, calming me and throwing me back into the pool of desire I've been drowning in for weeks. I can feel it when we reach the bank as he moves both of his hands to cup my butt, holding me tight to him as the water runs off us both, dripping to the grass below us.

"Where?" he asks, pulling my earlobe between his teeth and sucking it in between his soft lips, causing me to arch my back into him with the sensation rolling through me. I absolutely love when he does that.

I could care less right now where we make love. Why didn't I just stay in the water? Twisting to look over my shoulder, I spot our clothes strewn over the tree stump and turn back to claim his lips again, scratching my fingers up through his short hair.

"On our clothes," I say against his cheek, slowly squeezing myself along him and pulling my hips up, knowing it will drive him crazy. One of his hands shoots up my back and tangles in my hair, tugging my head back.

"You're gonna get it, Sweetheart," he almost growls, releasing my hair and kissing me hard while making it across the grass to our clothes in a flash.

I can feel him fumbling to toss them on the ground, and I laugh into his neck, thinking of how silly we must look right now. Two passion driven, love sick idiots. He's down on his knees, and I'm on my back before I know it with Bobby staring down at me, his eyes roaming my bare skin making me feel a tiny bit insecure.

As I'm moving my arms up to cover my chest his strong yet gentle hands stop me as his hazel eyes move up to my face. "No, don't do that," he says slowly leaning down to cover me, his weight a welcome thing as his warmth sinks into my wet skin. "I like lookin' at you," he whispers with a wink.

Pushing him back with my hand on his shoulder, I run my fingers down from his collar bone to his hip, tracing every single defined line along the way, which there is plenty of. Looking into his eyes I can't help myself and I bite my lip, moving my hand from his hip to wrap my fingers lightly around his shaft, feeling a shock of excitement run through my body just at its size. His eyes shut for a moment, snapping open to look at me with a whole other level of want. Squeezing just a bit and pulling my hand towards me, I twirl it around his cock and watch his eyes rolls back. He groans when I repeat the motion and I love the feeling that I get from pleasing him this little bit.

"I like the way you look at me," I whisper, leaning up and wanting him to kiss me. But he holds back, smiling that crooked little smile he does so well. As he lays over me again, he slowly, painstakingly pushes against my core; the sensation making my hands shake when I trail them up to grip his face.

"Please," I whimper out into his ear, not able to help myself as the thought of him inside me causes my body to tremble underneath him. I need Bobby like the flowers blooming next to us need the sun.

"Sweetheart," he whispers as he pushes slowly inside of me, stretching me as his hazel eyes keep contact with mine. "Tell me if I hurt you." He kisses me sweetly as I nod, wrapping my arms under his and pulling him tight to my chest. He is very big and when I squirm slightly, he stops, but I urge him on with sliding my hand down to his fine ass and squeezing.

I want him as close as I can get him, and as he

slowly starts to move within me, his lips never leave my skin. Whether they are covering mine or making a trail down my neck and across my chest, I'm loving every second that they are touching me. Moisture builds on my lashes as I look him in the eye again, but not from any pain.

"What's wrong?" he whispers against my lips, running his thumb along my cheek as the heat starts to coil at my core.

"Nothin," I gasp as my body reacts to my nearing climax, trembling while my hips rise and fall to meet his movements. My tears aren't from something that hurts but from something that feels amazing. This something that makes me feel whole and that nothing bad will ever happen to me again. This something is Bobby.

The way he's holding me with his arms just underneath me, propping me up gently to be in contact with every inch of his skin. The way he whispers my name with desire and emotion seeming to drip from every letter. The way his lips move over my skin and bring to life the sensitive flesh around my breasts, paying special attention to the spot on my neck that I told him about. He's making me feel amazing and as my climax rolls throughout my body, I'm sure I scare more than a few birds from the trees.

"So beautiful," he whispers, kissing my ear and then my cheek as I tighten the grip my legs have around his waist. I don't want this to end and I kiss him frantically, pulling his face to mine and not letting go until we're out of breath and sweating from the pace of our movements.

Drawing another climax from me with little effort, Bobby whispers, "My beautiful sweetheart," in my ear as he finishes. I hold him tight with my arms thrown over his neck, his cheek resting on my shoulder as our breathing is still heavy.

I can't tell you how long we lay there for, it seems like days, but as he shifts and pulls me onto his chest I see that the sun is close to being high in the sky, signaling noon is near. Lying full on top of him, both of us still naked, I rest my head on his shoulder, tracing a nonsensical pattern along his chest with my finger.

He's running his fingers through my hair and then trailing them down my spine, sending goose-bumps over my still sticky skin. I feel him take a deep breath in and release it, hugging me to him as he kisses my forehead.

"Never let me go," I say, not really meaning to say it out loud so it comes out as a whisper, but I mean it. Hell, what I really mean is *"Bobby, I love you. I know it's soon, but I really do. I need you every second of every day and it's not because we just had crazy, wild, mind blowing sex in the woods, it's because it's true,"* but I feel if I said that right now he might run away, calling me crazy. So I keep it in, scared to let it out.

He turns my face to him with his fingers under my chin, as gentle as ever, and his eyes roam over my face, a soft loving look on his face. He looks different right now. His eyes seem to be looking for something, moving from my eyes to my lips and back again. He leans his head forward, sweetly placing his lips on mine and kissing me with such passion I think my heart will explode right this second.

"I'll never let you go, Sweetheart," he murmurs, brushing his lips along mine again. "Never, Ellie…. Never."

# CHAPTER 9

## BOBBY

*May 28, 2013*

It's only ten after three in the morning and here I am, sitting in the pitch black living room with a cold sweat running over my body. I just woke up from another nightmare and this one was bad, probably the worst I've had yet.

I can still hear my team yelling for me to watch out, to get down and out of the way as a grenade flew into the room I was in. I can still smell the explosion and the dirt, feeling as if it's still pelting me in the face as I'm flying through the air. I'm thankful that when I shot straight up in bed it didn't wake Ellie. I can still see her feet tangled in the sheets from here, the moonlight streaming down through the open window in my room.

"God damn it," I curse, slapping my sweaty palms onto my forehead and rubbing them back through my newly cut hair. I don't want to feel like this and I thought maybe these nightmares were over, not having one in weeks, but as with a lot of things in my life I'm wrong. I rest my face in my hands with my elbows propped up on my knees, trying to let this fear and anger run its course in silence, but it's hard.

I feel the need to run it out, wanting to burst out Chad's front door and sprint down the street. I want to feel the pain in my leg that I haven't felt in a while. I want to blame this pain in my chest on it and push it aside. I want to scream and yell while punching something repeatedly.

Standing, I shake my arms out at my sides trying to let the tension roll through. I can't go back in there like this because I know I'll wake her. She's been here almost every night with me, driving me crazy with her smile and laugh, and then driving me insane with the way she whispers my name when we're making love. I've been on the verge of telling her I love her so many times within the last couple of nights that it's hard to keep it in. I'm afraid it will scare her and burst this awesome little bubble we have going on, so I'll keep it to myself.

164

The nights that she works at the bar I stay here alone, not sleeping very much, just lying in bed and staring at the ceiling fan while it spins around and around. I've offered to go over to her trailer and stay there, waiting for her when she got back, but she's turned me down every time, making me wonder why.

Is she hiding something? Is she ashamed of her home?

Well, she shouldn't be. I can care less if she lives in a trailer park. As soon as I get back on my feet I'm going to ask her to live with me, here in Wakefield. Where it's calm and peaceful, away from the noise and bustle of the city. Chad and I have talked about it a little; about me using the money I still have saved from when I sold my parents' farm to either buy or build a house.

It'll be nice. It'll be even better if Ellie is here with me.

A soft little whimper meets my ears and I turn to see her body shifting under the sheet, her arms flopping down when she rolls over then going up sleepily to brush the hair from her face. I can't help but smile at the scene before me as I lean against the door, my hands shoved in the pockets of my gym shorts.

She's so damn beautiful in the moonlight, the soft rays paling her skin even more than it already is. This pain in my chest makes me hate myself for wanting her, for wanting her to want me. I can't help but think that she deserves to be with someone else, someone whole and un-injured. Someone who doesn't have demons chasing them in the night, or night terrors plaguing them while they sleep.

She rolls over again as I sink down onto the cool

sheets, slipping my arm around her waist as her eyes try to open. "What's wrong, Bobby?" she mumbles as I pull her to me, holding her tight as I feel her leg drape over my waist, kissing her forehead and tucking it under my chin.

"Nothin', Sweetheart." I smile, kissing her forehead again and hugging her, relaxing at the sound of her content sigh. She mumbles something, but it's totally incoherent and I chuckle at her, rolling onto my back and tucking her into my side and loving the smile that's on her lips right now. If she smiles like that for the rest of my life, I'll die a happy man for certain.

I stare up at the ceiling fan while listening to her breathing even out. This is paradise I know for sure. Before, I was proud that I had a different woman every night come through my bed, but now, fuck that. I want her and only her. I want it like this.

I squeeze her tight and kiss her forehead one more time, closing my eyes as my lips linger on her skin. If only this moment could last forever.

A hand on my shoulder brings me to as the sun shines through the blinds and I act out of instinct, wrapping my hand around the wrist and turning. I feel another hand come behind my neck, trying to stay my motion as Chad's voice says, "Timmons, it's me. Chill!"

Looking up into Chief's face, I see the shock run over it and I release him, shoving my back against the headboard and kicking the sheets away. "Sorry Man," I mumble, running my hand over my face. Ellie isn't in bed and I look around the room as if she might be hiding.

"She's out on her run, lover-boy." Chief laughs,

tossing me a clean pair of shorts and a muscle shirt. He's already dressed for our morning workout in shorts and an old Navy t-shirt, leaning on the door frame and juggling a couple of water bottles.

"Well come on, boy," he says, nodding for me to hurry up and I throw my legs over the side of the bed, pulling my curved sport prosthetic from my dresser drawer. Switching the suspension sleeves while checking for irritation, I'm still fighting the sleepy morning feeling when I stand and follow him into the garage.

It's already hot and sticky at only quarter after seven. Today is going to be a scorcher. I yawn and start stretching my arms as Chad turns on the radio, switching it to the country station so that we can catch up on the local and national news while warming up.

I can see him get on the treadmill and crank it up, doing the normal Superman Chief speed, while I grab a medicine ball to do some lunges across the length of the garage and back, about one hundred times.

As the weather man talks about how it's going to be close to ninety-five today, Chad turns to me as I make the spin to go back, lunging down with the ball held up above my head and moving it down in front of me as I stand straight, switching legs.

"So you and Ellie seem to be getting' close," he says with a raised eyebrow, smiling when I give him a short laugh.

"You can say that." I smile, turning back again and speeding up my pace a little. We stay silent for a couple minutes and I finish my set of lunges as he turns the treadmill to a cool-down pace. I'm sweating like a pig and rip off my shirt, pressing the button near the ceiling to open the garage door and let in some fresh air.

'Close' isn't even breaking the surface as to how I feel about Ellie. I've never felt like this about anyone and it scares me more than a little. Chad clears his throat loudly and I know he wants me to elaborate. It's more like Rhea is bugging him, and I know Ellie doesn't spill that easy so Chad is her one source of info.

"Okay Man," I sigh, taking the pull up bar and whipping out twenty quick ones. "I think I love her. No, no. I *know* I love her." I'm holding myself up on the pull up bar as he turns to face me from the bench press, a wide smile on his scruffy face, and I could kick myself right now. I shouldn't have opened my big mouth, because I'm going to pay for it now.

"I fuckin' knew it," he shouts, pumping his fist in the air. I throw one of the water bottles at him, hitting him square in the side of the head. "Hey, watch yourself, kid," he warns, chucking the bottle back at me as he laughs some more. He's doing a little dance as I come up and sit down on the bench and he loads the weights on for me.

"It wasn't too long ago that we were all makin' fun of you for bein' head over heels, ol' man," I remind him, and he flips me off, sliding the last weight onto the bar.

Gripping the bar, I pull it free and test the weight, holding it straight above my chest. He's spotting me and Chad still has the shit eating grin on his face. I shake my head as I'm trying not to lose count.

"Don't open your fuckin' mouth to anyone," I

growl, bringing the bar down to my chest and back up again seeing the flicker of mischief in my friend's eyes. "Not Rhea. Not Reno. Not anyone…. got me, Chief?"

"Yeah, yeah." He rolls his eyes rubbing his hand through the short facial hair that is growing back from his last shave, and I shove the bar right up near his face, making him jump back and stare down at me. "Okay Timmons. Not a word."

"Good," I say, focusing back on my reps and finishing out when my arms feel like Jell-O. Sitting and taking the water bottle he offers me, I watch Chad as he walks over to the open door and leans out with his arms stretched up above him.

"If you break her heart…" He turns, his voice and demeanor cold and serious. The killer Chief I served with on SEAL Team Ten is in full force. "You break her heart and I'll break your body." His blue eyes cast a truthful shadow over me and I nod, knowing full well that every word he says is true. He will hunt me down and make me pay, but I have no intention of being on that end of Chief's anger any day soon.

"You don't have to worry, Chief," I assure him, and he nods, coming back over to shove me off the bench and take my spot.

As I stand and finish my water bottle I take in the calm of the dead end street Chad lives on. The hot temperature is settling a haze like fog over the houses, and as I move my gaze past Reno's, down the street, I see a patrol car parked in a driveway. It's not a local car, though, the colors are all wrong, but I can't see the side as it's facing up the street to see approaching cars.

"Chad? Who lives at that house down there?" I look over my shoulder and point to show him where I'm meaning, watching him squint and nod.

"Ol' man Pullman used to live there, but now he's in a home." He comes to stand next to me as I keep staring. I can swear that it's a Trooper car sitting down there, but I can't be sure from here. The haze makes it so that I can't even see the stop sign at the end of the street. If I had my rifle and scope I'd be able to tell what kind of car, the license plate, the driver's eye color and how many miles are on the car with the dashboard display.

"Why do you think there's a cop sittin' in the driveway?" A little ounce of fear trickles in, thinking that it's Ellie's ex, Jake, sitting there waiting for her to come running by and my muscles tense at the idea.

"I have no idea," he says, scratching his chin as I peek at him. I can tell his wheels are turning, and I can't help but let a wicked smile creep onto my face. He turns to me and says, "Wanna find out?"

I laugh. "Hell yeah."

In the matter of minutes we have our plan worked out and just like a well-oiled two man team we split off, Chad jogging calmly down the street as I sneak off to my left, over his mom's front lawn and behind the next house.

I skirt from backyard to backyard, tracking Chad as he makes his way at a very slow pace down the street toward the car like a normal, average, every day jogger. The haze gets thicker as we get closer, giving me a perfect cover that, as a sniper, I would have prayed for on a mission.

Getting into the backyard of the targeted house, I can hear Chief cough loudly, the signal to be ready, and I crouch behind a blooming hydrangea bush; peeking through the widespread branches. Waiting, watching; ready to spring into action to kick someone's ass.

~~~~

# CHAD

Approaching the car, I cough, signaling to Bobby. I can't see him through the haze so that means our little cop friend can't either and that's a good thing. Wouldn't want him running away before we get to have a little fun.

Sure enough, it's a Virginia State Trooper car, and as I round the trunk I can see there is only one occupant, sitting in the driver's seat with his feet up on the dash of the passenger side. I bang on the back door, scaring the shit out of him and he jumps. I come up to the window, tapping my knuckles on the glass.

"Mornin'," I yell, trying to act out of breath. The man has short dark hair so I know it's not Ellie's ex. From pictures and stories Rhea has shared, I know the bastard has blonde hair and he likes to keep it longer like I used to. I miss that hair.

The guy looks pissed and slowly rolls down the window. "Why the hell did you sneak up on me like that?" he yells, a red slightly creeping into his face as he looks me over. I'm about twice his build and could break his neck in a second, but he doesn't need to know that. "I coulda shot you."

"Ha, was just stoppin' in to say hello." I smile, trying to play it off like I'm being a friendly neighbor and good citizen, and the guy nods, shifting in his seat so I can see his name plate.

Walden. I'll file that away for later.

"Are you lookin' for someone?" I get back on topic, still jogging in place and looking around as if I'm trying to see what he's waiting for. Looking back into the patrol car I can see that he's been here for a while; the empty coffee cups and food wrappers covering the passenger seat giving him away.

"Speeders," he says sharply and it's a stupid lie. It's a dead end street and no one ever speeds down it, they know better. Sure, we get the occasional drunk idiot who is showing off, squealing their tires and revving their engines, but the street isn't that long to get up any real speed. But I just nod my head and keep jogging in place.

"Ah, well I was just goin' on my mornin' run and thought I'd say hello." I nod, acting like I'm going to turn away and keep running down the street into the haze, hesitating only when I hear noise coming from Bobby's position. I see him jogging toward us through the fog and turn to the Trooper whose face is paling by the second.

Ah, so he knows who Bobby is. Bingo.

He was watching and waiting for Ellie to come back through. The dumbass was probably sleeping the first time she went through. He straightens in his seat as Bobby saddles up beside me, nodding to him as if they were already acquainted. The kid is smooth, I'll give him that.

"Alright, well my friend and I are gonna get goin'. Have a good day," I smile and give him a wave as Bobby issues a weak, mocking salute, matching my stride as we turn away. Yards away we laugh to each other, hearing the cruiser crank to life.

"He knows who you are," I say, nodding toward the car as it roars by, barely stopping at the stop sign before squealing its tires and taking off, heading out of town.

"Yeah, and now he's runnin' away with his tail between his legs." Bobby smiles an evil little grin as we come to a halt at the end of the road, watching the tail lights disappear into the fog.

Bobby's cocky attitude has been known to get him in trouble, it has with me several times, and I just shake my head, slapping him on the back. Trooper Walden is running, but probably to go report to Jake and no doubt throwing wood on the fire, which could be bad for us. Not to mention bad for Ellie.

Turning back toward home we keep quiet until the garage when Bobby says, "Do you think we should go look for Ellie?"

Looking at the clock above my tool bench, I shake my head. "It's only eight, she'll be back soon." He nods, but I see him take out his phone and set it on the bench where he can see the screen from the floor.

Getting down on my knees beside him, I punch him in the arm. "Now, let's get our workout over with so we can go eat some breakfast with my wife and son."

He laughs and leans forward, taking the lead in our sets of pushups. I try and push the idea away, but I have this feeling that this isn't the last we'll see of Trooper Walden or his partner Jake.

That's okay. Let them bring it. I'm more than ready to see some action.

~~~~

*Ellie*

Taking my run into town today, I've said hello to a lot more people than normal, waving and smiling as I pass the morning crowd on the sidewalk going to and fro from the post office and diner. But the peaceful feeling of my run has been plagued. I've been bothered by this feeling that someone is watching me.

It started when I turned off of Rhea's road, but there weren't any cars on the pavement. Even now as I come upon Muncy's Pub, waving to Brad and Garth as they take a delivery, I feel this weird feeling and I quickly look over my shoulder seeing nothing out of the ordinary.

"You're losin' it, girl," I mumble to myself over the Halestorm song coming through my ear-buds. I must be going crazy, because there is no one following me; it's just silly to think so.

I'm just all stressed out over the situation between me and Bobby. We've been getting closer and closer, and I've almost told him I love him more than a handful of times but haven't gotten the words from my lips. I need to tell him my secrets before I tell him I love him. He needs to know who he's getting involved with.

I need to tell him that I was pregnant when I ran away from Jake and that I subsequently decided to terminate the pregnancy. He needs to know that I was and sometimes still am *that* afraid of Jake. He would have had total control over me and that child, turning our lives into hell. I just couldn't live with doing that to an innocent child and some will ask how I can live with myself knowing I killed an innocent child. It's a double edged sword and I'm still trying to deal with it myself.

Passing Muncy's Pub, I hear Garth whistle his normal call and wave again over my shoulder, taking a deep breath in and knowing my other secret I need to tell Bobby involves those two men. My night in Virginia Beach is something that I can't take back, I can't undo, and I need to own up to it if I'm to have a relationship with Bobby; which I'm hoping is the direction we're headed.

I'm still worried that I can't be what Bobby needs, but I'm determined to give him all of me, to be what I can for him and hopefully it will be enough. I can't help but let my eyes close for a second as I think of his lips on mine or grazing across my neck. My eyes pop open as a horn honks and I'm almost in the middle of the street.

"Sorry, Miss Paula," I yell, waving to the elderly lady in her 1980 Cadillac as I get back onto the sidewalk. She flips me off and goes roaring on toward the Legion, no doubt meeting her knitting group.

Taking a second and leaning my hip on a bench, I look around me. The quiet little town is sitting in a haze of muggy fog with its early risers mingling around. Trying to catch my breath from being scared half to death by that car horn; I shuffle my iPod to Jason Aldean and step back out onto the street. I lift my eyes to check for traffic and freeze in place.

A Virginia State Police car is sitting just on the edge of the fog, sidled up next to the hardware store. My heart picks up its pace and a tingling wave of fear starts to roll through my arms. I don't want to be afraid, but flashes of what used to be my life run through my mind just seeing the insignia displayed prominently on the side of that Crown Vic.

Getting back onto the sidewalk I try and act calm, making my way toward a side alley to skirt unnoticed out of the town center when a phantom pain strikes my jaw, causing me to flinch. My hand rubs the exact spot where Jake had struck me with the butt of his gun one night after drinking, taking his poker loss out on me while I screamed and begged for him to stop. Pausing for only a second by the alley, I look straight across the street at the patrol car; wishing I could see if there indeed is an occupant.

"I don't want to be afraid anymore," I say quietly to myself, turning and running down the alley without turning back around. "I'm not the weak little thing that I used to be and I never will be that woman again."

My pace is faster getting home than when I left, maybe from the fear and maybe from just wanting to see Bobby, but as I reach the front steps I feel like I might pass out and I plop down on the middle step, ripping my ear-buds out. This lingering fear has a hold on my heart.

"Are you okay, Ell?" I spin around as Rhea's voice finds me. She's standing at the door with Charlie on her hip, still in his pajamas and a slightly frightened look on her face. I nod because I'm still out of breath, and the look slowly disappears as she joins me, letting the screen door slam behind her.

"Your run lasted longer than usual," she says, sitting down beside me and putting her son square on her lap as he sucks his thumb, still not ready to be awake. Leaning back, I pull the tank up and over my head, basically peeling it from my sticky skin, and use it to wipe my face. I close my eyes and lean my face up, trying to cool off in this humid morning.

"Are you sure you're okay?" she asks again and I turn my face to her, my hair flopping out of its ponytail and sticking to my face as my cousin's stormy blue-grey eyes wash over me.

"I'm fine, Rhea," I say giving her a smile and reaching out to Charlie and tickling his side and getting him to giggle slightly and grip onto her chest tighter as if trying to be shy. "I almost got hit by a boat of a Cadillac, but I'm okay."

"Miss Paula?" She shakes her head as I nod and she laughs lightly. "That woman needs to have her license revoked or she's gonna kill someone." We both laugh at that one because it's true and I give my face a wipe one more time, desperately needing a shower to feel clean after this humid start to my day.

"Is breakfast ready?" I ask, taking Charlie from her and he wraps his legs and arms around me, snuggling his face into my neck like he always does.

"Is that all I am?" She throws her hands up in the air while getting up and following me as I hold the door for her. "Yes, Master; breakfast is ready, Master. Is there anything else you need, Master?" she jokes, rolling her eyes at me as I flap my fingers around her face, mocking her.

"I need another cup of coffee," is yelled from the living room and as we pass the hall closet I can see Chad with his coffee cup held high in the air. He's sitting on the floor, attentively killing aliens in Halo with Bobby sitting to his right and playing along.

"I'll give him a cup of fuckin' coffee," she grumbles to me, making me laugh, and stalks across the carpet yanking the cup from his hands and storming into the kitchen. Bobby looks back and winks at me just as Rhea returns, still acting like she's mad and she shoves the cup back into Chad's hand, turning back and leaving without a word. But I know she's laughing to herself right now.

"I love you, Honey," Chad yells, taking a sip of his coffee and making a loud lip smacking sound, setting the cup down on the table. "She's great, isn't she?" he says obnoxiously to Bobby, and I hear Rhea snort in laughter from the kitchen. These two are a hoot.

"Chad, you want me to put Charlie in his play pen?" I kiss the little boy on his forehead and put him down in the toy strewn pen as Chad nods. He smiles and gives me a little pudgy finger wave, his new thing, and I wave back then blow him a kiss.

Ducking into Bobby's room to grab some clean clothes, I almost run face first into his chest as I come back out into the living room. He has to catch me around the tops of my arms so that I don't fall backward and his hazel eyes smile down on me.

"Where ya headed, Sweetheart?" he says softly, leaning down and kissing my lips so sweetly that it makes my heart race. I almost forget what I was about to do.

"Shower," is all I say and it comes out as a whisper. Looking up at him, I see a mischievous grin fill his face as he winks at me. "What are you smiling about?" I ask, but in the blink of an eye I'm swept off my feet and on his shoulder, his hand finding my butt and smacking it loudly.

"We're gonna shower," he says, and I see Chad shaking his head at us.

I ask him for help, but he just makes a motion toward the screen, acting like he can't leave his game. But I'm not dumb. I can see he's still waiting to join in and I flip him off as we round the corner into the kitchen, heading for the hall bathroom near the basement stairs.

"Where do you think you two are goin'?" Rhea turns to us from the stove, the spatula still in her hand.

"Oh," Bobby stops, swinging around so that I can't see my cousin anymore, "we're just gonna get clean." He smacks my ass again and swings around in a hurry, making me laugh out loud and I can see Rhea making her way over to us, the spatula raised high.

"Oh no you don't, Timmons," she yells, swatting him on the shoulder and lower back as he tries to get us into the bathroom. "There is no hanky panky in

179

my shower." She yells, still hitting him as he laughs, trying to tell her to back off.

"Come on, Rhea, we have to get clean," he pleads, finally setting me down and winking at me again, but I just roll my eyes. My cousin is in full Momma Bear mode right now and I know she won't back down.

"You can get clean all on your own." She grabs his upper arm trying to yank him from the bathroom. It's a funny scene, seeing my petite cousin yanking this over six foot tall, crazy muscular man from the bathroom. She pulls him to just the other side of the door and stands so he can't try and re-enter. "Ellie is a big girl; she can scrub her own back."

I give him a little wave and slowly shut the door, trying to listen to his grumble as she swats at him some more. I can't help but laugh to myself as I turn on the water, thinking that my family is crazy. But I wouldn't want any other person to be my family other than Rhea because let's face it, we're two peas in a pod and I'm happy about that.

As I'm pulling on my shorts and tank later, I'm glad Rhea has central air because if I was in my trailer, I'd be sticky the second I stepped out of the shower and I would just walk around naked. No point in clothing when you have to fight to get them on, right? Stepping out and tossing my towel down the stairs, I help Rhea as she's putting the food on plates and setting the table.

"Alright ladies," Chad's voice booms through the quiet kitchen and we both turn to see him stretching while making his way to the table. He slaps his hands down onto his stomach and rubs his shirt back and forth, "I'm hungry as all get out. Where's my food, woman?" he jokes and Rhea scoffs.

I can't hold in the laugh as he winks when I put the juice and coffee on the table. Bobby's hand comes to my hip and I lean back into his chest as his arm drapes over my chest, holding me tight. His mouth brushes my ear as he moves to kiss my cheek and the smile that finds my lips is wide and happy. I lean over and peck him on the cheek, lingering there when he squeezes my hips with his strong hands. What can I say? The man makes me feel good.

"Here's your food," I hear Rhea snap, and I open my eyes to see her slam a plate down in front of Chad then turn and make for her own chair. He stops her, though, wrapping his large arms around her waist and pulling her down into his lap as she squeals and Bobby and I laugh. Charlie joins in from his high chair, squealing and giggling as my cousin and her husband continue to play around.

I'm surprised myself when Bobby's hands on my waist yank me down into his lap and pull my legs over so that I'm sitting sideways. His lips go immediately to my ear and light a fire in my heart as his hands slowly run over my bare legs, bringing goose-bumps to the surface.

"Bobby, quit it," I whisper as Rhea and Chad keep playing away and Charlie keeps up his squealing and banging his tray. He doesn't listen to me and one of his hands skirt up my thigh and tug at my knit shorts. If I had my way I'd rock his world right here right now, in this chair, but it's not my house so I open my desire closed eyes to see his roaming over my chest.

"Quit it," I say again, pushing his shoulder. He grins, snapping his gaze up to my face.

181

"You wanna take a ride with me after breakfast?" he asks, running a hand gingerly up my bare arm and tangling it in my hair, massaging my neck and effectively applying pressure to some pressure points he loves to utilize. It makes my body want to go weak and I see that evil grin reappear.

"Where are we gonna go?" I say, leaning my forehead against his and feeling as if we're the only two in the room. This right here is what I want. Just him and me being happy.

"Oh, you'll see." He smiles, kissing me sweetly and playfully nipping at my lips. I return the favor and he holds my head, kissing me deeply, sweeping his tongue along my lips and diving in when I open for him.

"Do I need to get the hose?" Chad's laugh breaks our little moment and I can see the same shock on Bobby's face that I know is running over mine. We were lost in each other for a second there. Looking to Chad, I see him raise an eyebrow as he releases Rhea and he holds his hands up pressed together, then slowly moves them apart signaling for us to separate.

"Okay, ol'man," Bobby jokes, kissing me quickly on the lips and pulling my chair closer so I can scoot in. I move just in time to miss a flying biscuit as it smacks Bobby square in the jaw, flaking and leaving a trail of crumbs on his face and shirt as it tumbles to the floor at my feet.

That set the tone for our meal, Bobby and Chad both throwing out insults and embarrassing stories and trying to upstage the other. Charlie follows his father's lead and tosses half of his food all over the place and Rhea makes Chad clean him up.

Drying the last dish as Rhea wipes the table I let

out a small scream as hands come to my waist and slip under my shirt, splaying out across my belly. "Ready to get outta here, Sweetheart?" his smooth voice and warm breath runs over my skin making it tingle.

I smile, wiping down the counter and then grabbing my purse. "Heck yeah."

Slinging the blue denim bag over my shoulder with Bobby's hand in mine, headed for the door, I say, "Say ya later cuz!" and hear Rhea toss in an okay as Chad nods to us from the stairs.

Bobby's truck is sitting on the street, looking like a redneck dream, and I smile while thinking to myself that it fits him to a T. It's an older Chevrolet Silverado Z-28, lifted up with running boards to help me step up and KC lights on the roof. It's a muted red color with some rust here and there and a pirate ship scene sticker on the back window. As I hop in, I peek in the back to see a picnic basket and blanket neatly stashed on the seat.

"Are we gonna be gone long?" I ask as he settles into the driver's seat.

"As long as you wanna be gone, Sweetheart." He smiles that wicked little smile and I can't help but blush. He grabs a pair of aviators and pushes them on, waggling his eyebrows at me.

"You're such a dork," I scoff, rolling my eyes and twisting to pull on my seatbelt when his arm encircles my waist, pulling me straight across the bench seat to be tight against him.

"Yeah, but I'm your dork," he whispers, his lips up against my ear. The sensation of his breath on my skin makes me shiver even in this heat. He kisses my cheek quickly, turning the key and bringing the truck to life.

It's not a quiet truck whatsoever and as we turn down the street he steps on it, squealing the tires and sending up a cloud of smoke behind us. I laugh as he yells a 'Yee-haw' out the window as we pass Kendall's parents' house and her father waves, shaking his head. I laugh at him as he sings along with the radio, turning his truck toward town and then out toward Spratley Cemetery.

As we get close to Harlan Dow's family farm, I lean my head on Bobby's shoulder and revel in his smell. His clean and masculine scent seems to run through my senses and attack my heart, making it jump up to a racing beat and I can't help but let out a sigh. He laughs a little and leans down; kissing my forehead lightly. I catch his chin with my lips as he moves his eyes back to the road. I could drive like this forever with this man, never having to stop for anything.

Lifting my gaze to the passenger window, I see the Dow's horses all out in the pasture, gathered together under the scattered trees and trying to stay cool. It seems like the both of us see Harlan on the tractor at the same time and as I lean out the window, waving to him atop his large John Deere bucket tractor, Bobby honks the horn. I can see Harlan smile, taking his cowboy hat off and waving at us as we pass, kicking up dust on the way toward the cemetery.

Parking his truck across the road from the Spratley driveway, Bobby turns to me with a smile. "Grab the blanket, girl, and let's go."

"Go where?" I look around and see a walking trail on our side of the road, but not much else. I vaguely remember the trail from when I was young, but I have no idea where he's planning on going.

After hopping out, I open the third door and pull the folded blanket out, shoving it in my bag as I see a Coleman cooler tucked away on the floorboard. He is planning on being gone for a while.

A smile creeps onto my face as I spy him standing at the front of the truck, stretching his long and muscular arms up above his head. The way his muscles show through that t-shirt make my mouth water and a million naughty little thoughts are running through my mind as I join him.

"We don't need the basket?" I ask as he takes my hand, tangling our fingers as his hand nearly encases mine. He doesn't know it, but the way he holds my hand really affects me. It's not just the skin on skin; it's that his big, strong hands can be so gentle and loving, breaking down the barrier that I normally put up around my heart. It's the way they blend so perfectly that sometimes I forget we're touching at all, as if we are connected there normally, all the time.

"No, we'll come back after we work up an appetite." He smiles, smacking my butt as we hit the grass, making me squeal and my face flush.

As we walk down the groomed trail he points out birds in the distance every now and then, our hands never leaving one another. There are tulips gathered together on the edge and I stop to smell them. They are my favorite, and as I turn back to Bobby with the two that I've picked, I see the handsome smile matched only by this amazing look in his eyes.

"What?" I say, parting our hands and walking in front of him with one of the tulips up to my nose. Spinning around and walking backward, I see that he still has that smile and look as he's slowly following me. He shakes his head, rubbing his hand over his chin and around to the back of his neck.

"Up over here is the spot I wanna show you." He points, obviously changing the subject, and I turn down the path where he indicates, watching as a family of rabbits goes darting off into the taller grass to my right.

Around an old Spanish moss tree I stop, taking in the wonderful scene before me. It's a creek surrounded by blooming flowers. Daisies, tulips, black eyed Susan's and little blue Forget-me-nots bathe this slow moving creek in beauty and I find myself just staring. His arms wrap around my waist and his mouth comes down to the crux of my neck, moving to my shoulder with a few light kisses.

"Do you like it?" he asks, his mouth lingering above my ear. This must be what he was doing with Chad the last couple of afternoons when they went to the 'hardware store' for hours. I nod my head slowly in response and he laughs. "Is that all I get after all that searching for an awesome spot for us? A nod?"

Without thought, I spin in his arms and take his face in my hands, planting my lips firmly on his. He did this for me? Making a spot for us? I don't know about you, but this makes my heart swell and I want to show him exactly how much I love this spot. I want to show him how much I love him.

As I nip at his bottom lip he lets out a soft moan, grabbing my face and tangling his fingers in my hair, holding my face to his as he kisses me deeply, effectively exploring me. He suddenly pulls away and I'm standing there stunned, my vision blurred from the desire coursing through my body. I feel him tug at my bag and realize that he's now throwing out and straightening the blanket near the base of the tree.

I can't move, though. I'm frozen in place with the sensation of Bobby's lips still lingering on mine. As he finishes tugging on the last corner of the blanket, he turns, a crooked grin on full display. Bringing my shaky fingertips up, I brush them along my bottom lip, the heat from his kiss lingering like the after burn of whiskey.

"Well come on, Sweetheart," he says, swiftly picking me up and kissing my lips. "Take a load off and relax."

As he sets me down I don't want his touch to leave me so I pull his face to mine again, kissing him as if I'm going to die if I don't. Tossing my purse off to who knows where, I place my hands on his cheeks and feel him drop down to his knees as he grunts.

"Are you okay?" I say, breaking the hold I had on him to peer down at his left knee, the worry immediately building within. His hand runs up my neck, tilting my face up so that we're nose to nose with his stare sending lightning bolts through my body.

"Sweetheart," he whispers, lightly running his nose along mine teasingly giving me tiny kisses letting our lips touch for only a second, "don't worry about me." He smiles, trailing kisses along my jaw and landing just below my ear. It scrambles everything I've been thinking about and all I want is him.

He wraps his arms around me as he claims my lips again, delving his hands up the back of my tank and pulling me up to him. I wrap my legs around his waist. I can't help but press my body against him, running my hands up his arms under the sleeves of

187

his shirt and across the muscles that I love so much. I can feel his fingers spread out as his hands move from my lower back to cover my shorts, pressing me tight, and I smile against his lips at how hard he already is.

As he leans slowly forward, my back gently finds the blanket, but I'm still ravenously searching him; roaming my hands under his shirt and all over his chest loving the way his muscles twitch as my fingers trace the defined lines. Sitting back up on his knees he smiles down at me, tugging his shirt over his head by the back of the collar and tossing it aside, giving me a great view as he closes the distance, kissing me teasingly. He's driving me crazy.

Pushing up against him, he stops moving, emitting an almost growl-like sound as he grabs my hips. He bites down on my bottom lip and I let out a small moan, a little from the slight pain but mostly from pleasure. Then I feel his fingers tugging at the button and zipper of my shorts. He yanks them down in one swift movement, laying me back down and losing no time in pulling my tank up and over my head, covering my mouth the second I'm free of the material.

"You okay, Sweetheart?" he asks as his thumbs slip under the lace of my panties, tugging them down slowly as he nips and sucks on my skin, smiling against my stomach right before dragging his tongue around my belly button. The only sound I can get out is a soft moan as the desire runs rampant through me. This man is killing me.

Coming back up, he smiles against my mouth, releasing me only so I can lean back as he finishes pulling my panties down slowly, keeping eye contact with me the entire time. In the shade of this tree Bobby sits back on his knees just looking at me. I squirm under his gaze, wanting his touch.

A sexy smile quirks up on his lips and he reaches his left hand out, barely grazing my face with his fingertips then slowly, agonizingly runs them down the length of my body, paying extreme attention to my chest. He's teasing and playing, that smile still on his face and I snatch his hand, trying to tug him down to me and fill this hole he's created with desire.

Sitting up and bumping my chest into his abs, I grab hold of the waistband of his shorts, yanking at the button, pulling them down to reveal his boxer briefs and the very evident fact that he's as turned on as I am right now. Lifting my face to peer up at him, I see the raised eyebrow and evil look in his eyes and it sends shocks over my skin again. It's like he has a hold on my reaction to him, commanding it to make me helpless to resist him.

"Oh Sweetheart," he smiles encircling my face with his arms and pulling me up, tangling his fingers in my hair as he holds me tight to him, kissing me deeply, "you drive me crazy."

I can't help but laugh a little at him as he lays us down, shucking his shorts and briefs in a blink. Running his fingers over my cheek and jaw, his hazel eyes roam over my face followed by a look that seems to be filled with pain or doubt and I grab his face, looking him in the eye.

"What's wrong Bobby?" I get out in a gasp of a question as I feel him situate himself between my legs, gently resting against my core. He kisses me sweetly, running his nose along mine and moving down my neck and chest, lighting another fire that feels like it

189

might consume me as he moves his way back up.

"Ellie," he breathes out, holding my face in his hands, "I love you."

Those three little words make my heart stop. He loves me? Did he really just say those words that I hold inside for him? I know the look on my face must be stunned and as his eyes roam over me, the smile starts to turn to a frown and I snap back to reality.

"*Tell him*," my heart screams as it kicks to a frantic beat, my chest heaving and falling in rapid succession. I'm afraid, but I can't let fear rule this moment.

"I love you, Bobby," I say, almost choking it out as a flood of tears rushes into my eyes coming out of nowhere.

There, I said it. I mean it from the bottom of my soul, but it's still hard for me to sit here and look up at him through blurry eyes, seeing a shock run over his handsome features. "I love you," I repeat as the tears spill out, running my hands over his face.

"I love you, Ellie." He smiles, kissing me lightly a handful of times. "I love you," he repeats with a smile, holding my face to his and easing down so that our bodies are connected. "I love you."

"I love you," I say into his ear as his lips move to my neck, wrapping my legs tighter around his waist because I never want him to leave me. I want this creek side scene to last forever just as I wanted our moment at the pond to last. This is different, though; it is more than the pond.

It is me and Bobby, making love without a care. We love each other. I love him and he loves me.

His touch has a different tenderness, his kisses linger longer and deeper, he whispers in my ear that he loves me every chance he has. I memorize every touch, pulling him tight to me and wrapping my arms over his chest as I feel my climax building.

"Sweetheart, I love you," he whispers in my ear, the lobe between his teeth as my climax rolls through me shaking my limbs and clearing my brain. I repeat the words to him and claim his lips, never wanting them to leave me.

Our moment doesn't seem to last long enough, but as he pulls me into his side I see the sun high in the sky, already past its noon position. I giggle into his chest. Time seems to slip away when I'm in Bobby's arms, but its fine by me.

The muggy atmosphere brings the afternoon bugs out and as they buzz and the birds chirp, I trace the lines on Bobby's chest; running my finger along his abs and up his sternum, moving across his shoulders to land on his pirate ship tattoo. It fascinates me, this work of art on his skin, and I climb on top of his chest, laying my cheek on his pec as I inspect it further.

The stormy seas, the ripped sails, and the 'Refuse to Sink' emblazoned on the bow giving way to the tiny peek of blue sky and calming land, letting him know safety is near. With my ear on his chest, listening to the rhythmic beat of his heart, I drill that little saying into my head.

"You're that clear sky," he says with his hand at the back of my head, turning it slowly so that I'm looking at him. I don't understand and he clearly sees it. A marvelous smile creeps onto his face. "You're that clear sky to my pirate ship. You're that safe harbor, that saving grace. My saving grace."

"Oh shush," I say, trying not to blush while turning my face away and he holds my head firm,

191

looking me in the eye. The look he's giving me says he's not kidding and it sinks in. He really loves me. He sees me as a happy point, a safe point. It scares me because he still doesn't know my secrets. Will he change his mind?

"Sweetheart, you're all that I want. No matter what, I won't ever let you go." He pulls my face to his, kissing me so sweetly that my heart breaks all over again and tears lightly find my lashes. I'm such a mess right now, but I'm happy and it's been far too long since I've been happy.

"I love you, Bobby," I say, kissing him again and he hugs me to him, holding me tight and running his fingers along my spine.

As we pull our clothes on a thought suddenly strikes me. I turn to him as he adjusts the suspension sleeve on his leg, replacing the prosthetic after straightening the tan material.

"What if someone came walking down here when we were buck ass naked?" I kind of yell at him and he laughs. It is kind of funny to think about and if someone had, they sure would've gotten an eye full. I laugh right along with him, standing and folding our blanket.

He just shakes his head and takes my hand, standing still so we can get one last look at our peaceful scene as we turn back down the trail. He has one of the tulips I picked tucked behind his ear as we make our way down the trail, bumping arms and smiling every now and then.

There is a different pressure on my heart now. A good kind. One that, at this moment, is making me a little light headed.

When we get out into the open I look up to see

his truck and, at the opening to the trail, a large orange cone. Cocking my head to the side I try and squint to read the black lettering.

"What the...?" I start to say as he starts to chuckle. We get closer and I see that the cone says, "Trail closed. Groomers Ahead".

"*Oh really?*" I think to myself, stopping in my tracks and giving him an incredulous look.

"Where the hell did you get that?"

"Chief gave it to me." He smiles, dodging my hand as I try and swat him. He wraps me up, kissing my cheek as I try and squirm loose. "I wanted us to have something special."

"Grooming special?" I scoff, turning my head away from him as he tries to kiss me. His fingers find my chin and hold my face still and I can't ignore his stare.

"No, you and me special," he says with a dead serious twinge of desire in his voice. His eyes tell me he's serious and I concede to his point, getting up on my tip toes and kissing him with my hands on his cheeks, dropping my purse and blanket. I love this man, and if he wants to use a cone to make sure we have a special moment, then why the hell not?

"I love you, Bobby," I say with more conviction, putting my forehead to his and hugging his neck. I love this man with all of my heart. It scares the hell out of me and it makes me giddy at the same time. I need him, I want him, and he loves me too.

"I love you, Sweetheart," he whispers, sweeping me up, grabbing my purse and blanket, and planting me in the passenger seat of his truck with another kiss.

This man is everything to me. He's my clear sky.

He's my safe haven. I hope I can be everything he needs me to be.

# CHAPTER 10

## BOBBY

*June 23, 2013*

"How many times have they called you?" Chief nods toward my cell phone as I silence it, throwing it back in the duffle bag at my side. It's going to be an awesome day today, and as Chad and I sit on the metal bench on the sideline of his old high school's football field making sure our sneakers are tied tight, I give him a laugh.

"A couple of times," I say, standing and making sure my shorts drawstring is tied and the belt with the red flags around my waist is straight. We are waiting on the guys from our SEAL Team, well our old SEAL Team, and we are going to have a nice, rowdy game of flag football.

The callers Chad is questioning me about are private contractors, mercenaries, who have been calling me night and day bidding for my attention. Private security companies who are hired by the government to help them out overseas.

They know I still got it. Taking my leg doesn't take my shooting capability away and all of my doctors say I'm healing faster than they thought I would, which is awesome. With every message these soldiers of fortune leave me, they raise the stakes, offering me more and more money; more perks. One has even gone so far as to offer me a brand new car in return for my four year agreement to employment with undeterminable deployment times.

It's something I'm thinking about, due to the fact that I can't rely on this country's government to take care of me as they don't take care of the Veterans now. It's a shame and it pisses me off, but I won't let it dampen my mood right now. The day is too promising for that.

Looking down the sideline, I spot my Ellie looking all cute in her shorts and tank top with the blue flags tied at her waist. She's laughing and joking with Rhea, Rosa, and Kendall; all of them playing and cooing over Marisol and Charlie, who are crawling around in the grass.

God I love her. I can't help but stare at her, a goofy smile caressing my face when she bursts out in laughter to something Kendall says.

"Hey! Romeo," Reno yells, slapping the back of my head and I turn on him, shoving him with both hands and watching him fall over from his precarious position of one leg on the bench tying his shoe, to lying on the ground swearing. Bursting out in laughter my rant is short lived as he gets up, the look on his face causing me to jump up and sprint in the other direction, this angry man on my heels.

"Come on, Reno." I laugh, keeping ahead of him and swerving around the field, dodging his hands and feet as he attempts to tackle or kick me. "What's wrong? NCIS make ya soft?"

"You have an unfair advantage," he huffs, and over my shoulder I see him stop and throw his hands up. I jog to a stop about ten yards away, turning and winking at him. "You have a robot leg. It's unfair." He breathes and I throw my head back, letting out a good chuckle as I throw my arm around him.

"You always got an excuse, Reno," I say, slapping him in the chest and he flinches. In the blink of an eye his arms tighten around my waist and I'm flat on my back, staring up at the sky; a victim of a hip toss with Reno's smiling face peering down at me.

"Never let your guard down, kid," he says with a smile and a wink, his dark eyebrows waggling. "Especially when you're around me and the Chief."

I'm still in a state of minor shock as he walks away, and I can hear Chad's distinctive laugh echoing through the early afternoon air. I'll always be the 'kid' to those two. I laugh to myself, recounting my miscalculations of Reno's attitude and the moment I knew he was going to retaliate. Next time I'll get his ass, he just won't see it coming.

Sitting up and lazily wrapping my arms around my bent knees, I squint in the sun to see my SEAL teammates getting out of their trucks and Jeeps in the parking lot. Today will be the first day since waking up in the base hospital that I will see any of my brothers. Uclid was the last one I saw as they wheeled me out to a chopper, bound for yet another hospital, and that had been only hours after I had woken up and been told what had happened. We have a lot to catch up on and the thought of joking and carousing with them brings me jumping to my feet and jogging across the grass.

"Timmons." My old LT, Austin French, smiles, throwing his hand out and grasping mine tightly and pulling me in for a one armed hug as is the usual greeting. I hug him tight. It's good to see his dumbass smile and scruffy un-kept beard. "You're lookin' good, brother."

"Thanks French. You too," I say genuinely as his blue eyes roll and he lets out that loud, annoying laugh he's famous for, making everyone around us laugh as well.

I shake hands and hug Black, Benson, and Talbot, joking and laughing with them all, leaving my spotter and best friend, Uclid, for last. His shorter, stockier build is standing here before me with a dumb smile on his face, shaking his head at me.

"Well, you mother fucker." He laughs, taking my hand and pulling me into a hug. His smile is a great thing to see and I laugh as he pats my back extremely hard as his usual style. "Lookin' good, bro." He smiles, releasing me.

"Shut the hell up," I scoff, slapping my hand on his cheek and squeezing his face. "I've missed ya, bro.

It's good to see ya."

"Yeah, you don't call, don't write," he says in a fake girly voice, putting his finger to his chin and I push him back, chuckling at him. "Oh wait. I was in fucking hell so you couldn't write or call, my bad!"

As we settle into conversation, we circle up with Chad and Reno, all of us joking and laughing and I know nuns would be saying a million prayers for us with all of the curse words flowing through the wind right now. Harlan, Garth, and Brad join us, flawlessly mingling with the conversation and adding their own quips and jokes and I'm speechlessly happy right now. I'm surrounded by my friends, my Team, essentially my family. Chad had been right; this *is* something that I need.

"Are we gonna play football, or are y'all just gonna sit there and shoot the shit?" I turn from my conversation with Elliot to see Ellie standing just a few feet away, her blue-green eyes trained on me as her hand finds her cocked hip.

Damn, she is sexy as hell and her presence makes me go from bullshitting with the boys to thinking naughty thoughts about her in a split second. Knowing there is a mischievous look displayed on my face, I stand and make a lunge for her, scooping her up in my arms as she squeals and wraps her legs around my waist.

Just the feel of her close to me brings a smile to my face and makes my heart race; her giggling in my ear making me want to run off and have my way with her in the backseat of my truck. I laugh lightly. Her lips on my cheek and some rousing from behind me make me turn, shifting her in my arms and settling them underneath her butt, cradling her to me. In this second I don't want to ever let her go.

"I see you finally did it," Elliot says, smiling from ear to ear and I shake my head, knowing the jokes that are about to follow throughout the day now.

Ellie gives me a questioning look with a smile, and I laugh, pulling her face to me with one hand while crushing her body along my torso with the other as her legs squeeze my waist tight. As I release her lips she asks, "What is Uclid talkin' about?"

"You, Sweetheart." I grin, kissing her lips one more time, then her nose and then setting her down, immediately missing her weight and presence once her feet are on the grass. "He's sayin' how I finally got you."

"Yeah, after all the belly achin' and day dreamin'," French chimes in and all the guys laugh at my expense. After flipping them all off, I grab the football off of the bench and throw it as hard as I can at French, causing him to stop laughing and huff as it hits him in the gut and he wraps his arms around the ball to keep from dropping it.

"Is that all you're gonna do, run your mouth, or are we gonna play some ball?" I taunt, giving the LT my cocky attitude that I know he hates. The commander in him likes his guys to be complaisant and I was never one to reform to that too much. His blue eyes turn into slits as he glares at me.

"Oh, you're gonna get it, boy," he says, giving me an evil grin as he tosses the ball over to Chad.

All I can do is laugh, adrenaline coursing through my veins at the anticipation of a good game. Jogging backward out onto the field I watch as my SEAL brothers pull on their flag belts, French purposely picking blue to be on the opposite team from me, and

I grin, yelling for them to hurry up as Chad and I make it out to the fifty yard line.

Chad hands the ball off to Reno, nodding for him to kick it down the field to the blue team who are congregating and mingling. I can tell French is running his mouth about me as Ellie giggles, telling him to be quiet, and I smile. *"Oh just wait, French,"* I think to myself, nodding to Chad when he asks if I'm ready.

"Are you guys ready yet?" he yells down the field as he straightens Rhea's flag belt, kissing her nose and patting her butt as she walks away and joins Rosa on the far end from me. He doesn't care what anyone thinks about his displays of affection and hell, neither do I. Let the guys make fun of me; at least I have a woman when I go home.

"Yeah," French shouts, and I see Black and Benson nod along with him, "bring it."

"Oh hell yeah," Elliot shouts beside me and Garth slaps him on the back. We are all ready for a little fun, and I know my SEAL brothers are going to use this time to get some stress out. I'm ready for it too.

Reno kicks the ball down field and we're off after it, my focus is on the balls path in the sky. Hearing Ellie yell out that she's got it makes me laugh to myself, zoning in on her location and I wave to Uclid to fan out to my right, planning on him circling around beside her in case one of the guys gets in my way.

Now we have a loose rule for flag football. If the girls weren't here it would be full on tackle, but with the girls we can't do that so for them we'll pull the flags. As for us guys, we're fair game to tackle and that's perfectly fine with me. I played ball all through high school and we use to play pickup games when we could overseas.

I see Ellie catch and cradle the ball and I'm only a few yards away, smiling when she looks up to see me. She squeals, taking off to her left as Harlan tries blocking for her and takes out Uclid. It was a good, clean hit and as I hurdle over them lying on the ground Ellie is running full out toward the end zone.

"You better run faster, Ellie Mae," I tease as I catch up to her, tapping her on the shoulder.

"Oh no you don't, Timmons," I hear from my right and am hit with what feels like a train, pushing me to the ground and my breath leaves my chest, hearing French's deep chuckle from on top of me. I see his blue eyes peering down at me, a smile plastered wide on his hairy face as he gets up from the grass.

"Told ya you were gonna get it." He laughs, jogging off as I sit up, seeing Ellie doing a touchdown dance down in the end zone. Her scoring doesn't make me mad because hell, any guy would love to see his girl shaking it like she is right now, but I grip the grass in anger, anyway, mad at myself for being tackled.

A group of motorcycles roar in the not so far off distance and as I get to my feet I see Ellie's smiling face looking right at me. She sticks her tongue out and shakes her butt some more and all I can do is laugh, enjoying the moment.

"Shoulda snatched my flag when you had the chance," she taunts as my team joins me, ready for the blues to kick off.

"Just wait, Sweetheart," I yell back, waving my hand up in the air when Black asks if we're ready. *Oh just wait.*

When the football hits the sky, Uclid and I split from our side by side position making it so that Rhea or Rosa can catch the ball and run with it. It ends up landing in Rhea's arms and with her right beside me and Chad on the other; we make our way down the field. I pull one of Kendall's flags, halting her path for Rhea and she yells at me but I laugh it off, waiting for the next.

French's laugh gives him away before I see him break from behind Black, whom Uclid takes down flawlessly, and I zero in on him. Just like if I was looking through my scope at a high value target, I see nothing but French. I'm adjusting my movements for his and as Rhea scoots off to my right, dodging French's attempt, I take him out at the waist, wrapping my arms around his back and driving him down into the warm grass and hearing his wind gush out.

Bouncing up onto my knees I see my team gathering up and Chad helping Reno to his feet, the ball on the ground and ready to be hiked. I look down at French, smiling my ass off as he flips me off.

"Better get up, ol' man." I laugh, jumping to my feet and offering him my hand which he slaps his into, grasping my fingers tighter than needed and rising to stand right up in my face.

"I'm glad you're yourself, Timmons." He smiles, patting me on my back as we turn to join the others. I smile at his words, letting them sink in. I still have my moments, but I'm doing better.

"Yeah, I'm glad too," I say, pushing him lightly as we reach the others and rejoin our teams. I'm happy to be feeling better about my life now, being an amputee. I know that I wouldn't be able to do this without Chad, Reno, Rhea, Rosa and their friendship.

Ellie, well Ellie is my clear sky. As I look over to her, roaming my eyes over her dark hair and pretty smile, I can't help but let my heart race to a new beat, ignoring the adrenaline from the game and running on her love alone.

Huddling up with Chad telling us he's going to throw to Elliot for a possible touchdown, we all spread out on the line of scrimmage. Brad lines up with me, being about the same build and height, and I talk a little smack; which he dishes right back, making me laugh.

Reno snaps the ball to Chad and it's on. I drop my shoulder, throwing the advancing Brad up and over. Out of the corner of my eye, I can see him drop to the grass on his back rolling and getting to his knees, swearing loudly at me and I leave him behind, watching as the ball sails right for Uclid, heading for the end zone.

Just as I think the ball is going to land in Elliot's arms, Ellie pops up out of nowhere and snatches the ball from its path and then sprints in the opposite direction. I stop in my tracks, as do most of the guys and for a split second I'm not really sure what to think. I can hear her laugh as Rhea and Rosa go chasing after her and we just watch her with our mouths open.

"Well hot damn," I mutter to myself and take off after her. I must have spurred the other guys out of their state of shock because as I run by, they all join in, tackling one another as I try and catch up. I pass Rosa just as Kendall rips one of her flags out and I return the favor, tossing Kendall's flag up in the air as

I sprint past.

Rhea is right on Ellie's tail, both of the girls laughing as I catch up. Rhea sees me and stops running, throwing her hands up in defeat. We're only yards away from the end zone as I wrap my arms around her waist, hearing her scream in shock as I try to pull her up but lose my footing.

Trying to cushion her fall, I twist onto my back so that when I connect with the ground she's pressed against my chest, her head bouncing off my shoulder. Holding her tight I see the ball rolling off, out of her arms and I can't help but laugh, squeezing my arms around her as she tries to squirm free.

"Dang it, Bobby," she says, turning to face me as I feel her legs slip to either side of my waist, "I almost had another touchdown."

Her fingers find my chin and shake my face as I laugh some more, not letting her get up as I try and sear her skin to mine by squeezing her even tighter. Her knees tighten on my sides and I pull her face to mine, running my nose along hers because I know it teases her.

"I could punch you right now," she mumbles with a smile, kissing me with such force that she pushes me back against the grass, her fingers raking through my hair but I'm not complaining. I freaking love it. She has the best kiss that I've ever experienced, and as her soft lips glide over mine I feel that ever present need for her rising within. I know we better quit before I have a very evident giveaway in my thin gym shorts to how she's making me feel right now.

"Oh well, isn't that cute," a condescending, deep voice comes from behind me and Ellie acts like she's been struck by lightning, separating our lips and sitting up. I see a painful fear cross her expression and get up on my elbows, peering over my shoulder to see a group of guys standing just inside the end zone with our football in a blonde man's hand.

Easing Ellie off of me and flipping over to my knees, I get a good look at the blonde man standing before me, tossing the football from hand to hand with a fast spiral. His hair is tied in a ponytail at the base of his skull and his green eyes are intent on Ellie, his bearded face displaying a nasty little smile.

As my breathing from the sprint to catch Ellie slows, I look over to her to see her eyes on the grass with her shoulders slumped and it dawns on me. I know this guy. Looking back to him I stand quickly, my muscles tensing as his eyes meet mine.

"Jake," I say, not trying to hold in the cool, deadly meaning behind it. What the hell is he doing here?

As I help Ellie to her feet that smile returns to his lips, causing my gut to twist, my fist clenching on my free side and I pull Ellie into me, cradling her into my left side as I see Chad and the others come up and join us.

"Navy boy," Jake says in a thick Southern boy accent, spitting on the ground and tossing the football to one of his buddies behind him. "I haven't had the pleasure of meeting you. How is my wife treatin' you?"

Just the tone behind his words makes me grind my teeth and feel the need to bust his teeth, but as I make my move to step forward Chad places a hand on my arm, shaking his head as I look at him. Looking from Chief to Ellie, I see the hurt and fear playing openly across her features, her lips quivering as she holds one of her hands up to them.

Suddenly she bursts out and says, "What the hell are you doin' here? What the fuck could you possibly want?" She pushes past me and I can tell she's running on adrenaline from the fear, her arms shaking as she clenches her fists at her sides, stopping just feet in front of her ex and his leather clad friends. They must have been the motorcycles I heard not too long ago.

"Oh Ellie," he laughs as I come up behind her ready to knock out anybody who comes close, "your little mouth is gonna get you in trouble."

"You can't touch me," she screams as I see her scan his group of buddies, settling on the man who had staked out Chad's road in the patrol car. "None of you can, because I'm not gonna take it anymore. I'm not afraid of you."

"Oh yeah," he says, his eyebrow quirking up. I just want to body slam his ass, choking him out until he cries for his momma. As he reaches into his leather vest, I step in front of Ellie, ready to shield her from a possible gunshot as Chad and the guys join me. Jake is a cop, he has the right to carry a gun, so I don't know what he's reaching for. But as a wide smile plays across his face, he laughs, pulling out an envelope.

"Whoa boys," he laughs and his friends join in. If they only knew how many buttons they were pushing with all of us they'd wipe those dumbass smiles off their shitty faces and quit playing games. "No need to jump. I jus' wanna show lover boy here what his little sweetie has been hiding from him."

Hiding from me? What the hell is he talking about?

Looking down into Ellie's eyes, I see the fear come to life again and it makes my heart hurt. She can't be hiding anything from me, can she?

~~~~

## Ellie

Oh no, no, no.

This can't be happening right now. When I see the question in Bobby's eyes I have to look away, shifting my gaze back to my son of a bitch ex and his shit eating grin. He winks and I look to the envelope in his hand, looking like it has something like papers or pictures within it.

"I haven't been hiding anything," I grind out, trying to call his bluff and maybe he'll back off, but he just smiles, reaching his hand into the manila envelope and pulling out a stack of photos. My heart stops and I know my face is displaying the horror of the situation.

"I beg to differ." He grins, dropping the envelope and thumbing through the pictures, showing them to his Trooper friends and making them laugh.

"Hey, Navy boy," he yells, picking out a few pictures and tossing them out toward us. They land only inches from Bobby's feet. I should bend over and pick them up before he does, but I'm so nervous that I can't move. I'm frozen, "take a look at those."

Jake nods to the pictures, and from the corner of my eye I can see Bobby look at me before he bends over and picks them up. My heart feels as if it might explode from my body as he straightens slowly, his eyes trained on the pictures.

"Did my wife tell you that she strips at that club she works at?" I can't help but gasp a little as Jake's words hang between us like a thick fog. Everyone is silent except for him, his little chuckles of delight and victory acting like knives to my heart. "God only knows what else she does with the scum that goes in and out of there."

"Ellie?" Bobby's soft whisper rips through that fog like a missile aimed for my heart, and as I look at him, the disbelief on his face brings the tears to my lashes. He's shaking his head slowly as he looks back at the pictures and I can just imagine what they have on them. I don't need to see them.

One of me up on the pole. One of me doing a split provocatively. One of me shaking it and rubbing my chest on some guy's face. Yeah I'm not proud of it, but I had to pay my bills and Jake had made it impossible for me to work anywhere else except for the temping at the attorney's, but that was few and far between.

"I'm sorry, Bobby, I meant to tell you. It just…" I try to explain, but the hurt on his face makes the tears flow freely down my cheeks and Jake interrupts me.

"Oh shut up, *slut*," he says harshly, throwing some more pictures out and they scatter on the grass. "Explain those." He nods to one that landed closest to me and hesitantly I pick it up, flipping it over and flinching at the image.

It's the night in Virginia Beach. He must have followed me, why didn't I think of this? Why was I so stupid? As I stare down at the image shot through the hotel window of me sitting on Garth's lap, naked, with Brad kissing my neck from behind I feel like throwing up. Crumpling the thick paper in my hand, I toss it to the ground and look up at Jake, anger flowing through my chest making it hurt with tension.

"What the fuck?" I hear Bobby exclaim, and then I see him toss the photos to the ground.

"Hey, Man, don't over react." I see Garth throw up his hands in defense as Chad and Reno grab Bobby's arms, stopping him from advancing. It's not his fault. It's not Brad's fault either. I slept with them, it was my decision and I can't take it back. Now it might ruin everything.

This can't be happening. Everything is falling apart. My hands come to my chest as Bobby continues to yell at Garth and Brad, swearing and calling them names as Jake just stands there smiling. He's smiling.

"One more thing, Navy boy," he says, and Bobby spins around, his face red from anger. His chest is heaving in and out and to me, it looks like he might explode.

"I don't want to hear one more fuckin' word from your god damn mouth," he grinds out and shakes Chad and Reno off, giving me a hard look that breaks me down, causing my legs to tremble.

"Oh no, you see, you want to hear this one, it's the most important." Jake's attitude changes from happy and gloating to hatred as he looks at me and I know what's coming, but I can't get the words out to try and protest, to try and stop him. "Ellie is a baby killer."

"What?" the first reaction comes from Rhea, somewhere behind me but I can't face her. "Ellie, what is he sayin'?" she asks. I'm still frozen in place, my body shaking from the combination of anger, fear, and devastation as my life falls apart at the seams.

"What I'm sayin', *bitch*," Jake chimes in, no doubt pissing Chad off, "is that your cousin is a baby killer. She killed our baby. She had an abortion, not caring what I wanted."

Silence surrounds me as I continue to try and hold in the massive sobs that want to break out. I can feel everyone's eyes on me and it makes my skin crawl.

"I hate you," I whisper, looking at him slightly as he stands there in his leather with his security blanket of goons. "I *hate* you. You will *never* deserve to be a father." My voice rises as I raise my head, looking this green eyed devil straight in the face and coming within a foot of him.

"Yes, I stripped. But only because you took every other opportunity of employment away from me by threatening the employers," I yell right in his face, not caring that the tears are streaming down, and I poke him in the chest. "Yes. I had the abortion, but only because I didn't want you to expose an innocent child to the life you had given me. I didn't want you to get mad because they didn't wipe the table right and continuously whip them with your belt for three hours, or punch them in the face and break their nose when they drop the salt shaker and get salt on the counter." He's smiling at me again as I recount only two of the numerous times he beat me.

Spinning around, I face Bobby, Rhea, and my

friends, their faces still displaying mild shock and the sobs creep from my chest. I bunch my shirt between my fingers as those hazel eyes roam over me, displaying anger and disgust where they, only minutes ago, had shown love and want.

"I'm sorry I lied," I choke out, feeling the need to run away just like I had the last night in West Virginia. "Everything is true and I'm sorry. That's all I can say." Bobby is shaking his head, not meeting my gaze as everyone else is looking to each other, no doubt trying to make sense of the scene they just witnessed.

"Ellie, I don't know," Bobby starts to say as Jake's hands find my waist, his lips brushing my earlobe.

"He doesn't love you anymore, *slut*," he says harshly as I try to squirm from his grasp, digging my nails into his arms and hearing him swear. I feel his boot meet the back of my knee, and I cry out as I hit the grass. "He doesn't want some damaged slut. Get up bitch."

I don't turn around. I don't look over my shoulder. I just get to my knees and then to my feet, running toward home. Running and crying, not paying attention to the sound of my name being called out behind me. Everything is ruined.

I ruined it all. I am so fucking stupid. I mucked it all up, and now I don't know if I can fix it. Jake is right. Bobby won't want me now. So I run, turning out of the parking lot and heading for the trailer park at a break neck pace.

I'm not stopping at any of the stop signs or crossroads, let a car or tractor trailer hit me, I don't care. As I sprint into the trailer park driveway, I'm falling apart from the inside out. The sobs are wracking my body as I reach my steps, but I don't care if any of my neighbors see me. Let them look and gawk, wondering what the hell I'm doing as I throw open the door and then slam it shut, shaking the walls and knocking some of my frames to the floor.

"How could I be so stupid?" I scream, dragging my arm across my counter and pushing everything to the floor. I can't do this. Sinking to the kitchen floor with my back against the cabinets, I shove my face into my knees.

I should have just told him right out. I should have told him everything, leaving no rock unturned, and then this little episode wouldn't matter. But no, I didn't do that because I'm weak. I'm weak and stupid, and now look at my life; I've ruined everything with Bobby and probably with Rhea.

My cell phone rings, but I just yank it from my pocket and throw it across the room, hearing it shatter at the same moment I hear the distinctive rumble of a Harley engine. I should have known he would come here. It isn't like him to leave business unfinished.

The screen door opens and slams shut, his motorcycle boots clicking on the linoleum floor, and then I can feel him looming over me. Wiping my cheeks with my hands, I look up at him, seeing a smile across his lips the same way he would before I'd be blamed for something I didn't do.

"Hello, Ellie Mae," he says, smooth as whiskey, unbuckling his belt and slowly pulling it from the loops. The leather makes a loud, ear piercing snap as he stretches is between his hands, warming it up.

"Hello Jake," I say, getting to my feet with the help of the counter. This is going to end. This is going to end with me standing my ground.

~~~~

# BOBBY

What the hell just happened?

As I watch Ellie run off, crying, not yielding to Rhea's screams for her to come back I'm in shock. Is this a fucking nightmare? It must be. French must have knocked me out on accident when he tackled me and I'm dreaming, that's all.

"What do ya think about her now, Navy boy?" the deep voice meets my ears again and I turn my face away from Ellie's disappearing form to face this blonde son of a bitch. He's smiling and laughing, elbowing his buddies as if he just did something smart and it irks me beyond belief.

Without thinking, with those pictures of Ellie up on the stripper pole, half naked and having sex with Garth and Brad flowing through my mind, I stalk right up to this laughing son of a bitch, the anger flowing like blood in my veins. I wind back and plow my fist right into his mouth, loving the feel of the pain as it shoots up my arm and he stumbles back.

"What the fuck?" I hear murmured from one of the goons as Jake spits blood onto the ground and it's on. I'm bombarded by two or three of them, blocking and throwing punches, wrapping my arms around one of their waists and tossing them to the ground as another asshole kicks at my back. I don't feel it. I'm too angry to feel right now.

I see Chad and the others join in the rumble, tossing guys and punching them, Reno knocking one out with a single punch, but my vision is zoned in on Jake and his goddamn smile. I'm going to break that smirk off of his face if I get to him.

"Come here, boy, and let me give you some of your own medicine," I yell, blocking a haymaker from a burly man. Returning the favor, I nail him right on the bridge of the nose; shattering his sunglasses as the blood gushes out and he falls to his knees.

Looking back up, I see Jake and his little shadow, Walden, hightailing it toward the parking lot and I'm immediately sprinting off after them. There is no way they are getting away.

"What are ya runnin' for?" I yell, catching up with Walden and Jake as they just hit the black top. I reach out and yank on Walden's leather vest, pulling him to the ground, but when I turn to get Jake I see him getting on his motorcycle.

"Maybe next time, Navy boy." He laughs as his bike roars to life and he speeds off. I chase him a short distance, the adrenaline and anger rolling through me like water over a waterfall.

My chest is heaving and hurting with everything that has been thrown at me, and I turn back toward the field, spotting Walden trying to get up from where I had tossed him down. I'm going to make someone pay for all of this pain I'm feeling right now; for pulling down the perfect picture of a life I was starting to build.

"Oh no you don't," I growl, running over and planting my right foot in his gut, loving the sound as the wind rushes out and he falls to his side. "You think you can just come over here an' throw shit in my face then run? I'm no pussy," I yell, kicking him again before dropping down to my knees, trapping him, and driving my fist into his face, hearing the crack and pop of bones.

I don't stop; I hit and strike him, seeing the blood flow down onto the black top. I can't stop. I'm not only hitting this man for me, for my anger, but I'm hitting him for Ellie, too. For all she went through at the hands of this man's friend. The nights she cried herself to sleep with welts and bruises. For the moment she had to decide to have the abortion to keep a child from having a hellish life and maybe turning out like their father.

"Timmons," I hear in the fog of my anger, but I keep hitting, hearing a gurgle travel up from the man beneath me. I feel hands wrapping around my arms, stopping their movement and I'm yanked to my feet. "Bobby!"

I hadn't noticed that my breathing was heavy, but as I turn to face Elliot, my mouth is open and I'm struggling for breath. The anger is still raging through me and my arms are shaking as I look down to my hands, seeing them cut and covered in blood. As I look around, my brothers surround me, all of them breathing hard from the fight and a couple with bloody lips.

Brad is kneeling next to Walden, calling 911 as I see Jake's other men limp to their bikes, getting on and roaring off in the opposite direction that Jake went. Then it hits me. Where the hell is Ellie? Shucking the hold on my arms, I swing around, my anger dissipating a little replaced by some fear.

"Where's Ellie?" I yell, looking to Chad and seeing him comforting Rhea and the crying Charlie. Rhea has tears running down her cheeks and they pull at my heart. Ellie is probably crying right now, too. She needs me.

But she lied. How could she lie to me like that?

Looking over to Harlan and Kendall, I ask again, "Where's Ellie?" my breathing hard and heavy, my chest rising and falling in rapid succession.

"She ran off." Harlan points off in the distance and I can't believe that I let her run off. I should have acted differently. I should have listened to her when she was saying she was sorry.

"I need to go after her," I say, pushing past Chad and he reaches out and grabs my arm, his blue eyes locking onto mine with a hard look.

"I don't think that's a good idea," he says quietly. "Give her a little time."

"Ha," a gurgle of a laugh comes from Walden still lying on the ground and he grabs for his face, groaning in pain. "You're too late, Navy boy. Jake's probably already got her."

"What did you say, ya piece of shit?" I stalk over to him, squatting down to hover over his face. He looks up at me, trying to smile. He tries to laugh and ends in a cough, groaning some more, and I'm not going to lie, it makes me smile that he's in so much pain physically. It matches what I'm feeling inside.

"You think we came here just to piss you off?" he grumbles, and I can hear the ambulances off in the not-to-far off distance. "He came here for her. And

218

he's probably at her dump of a trailer now, teachin' her a lesson. Givin' her what she deserves."

No, I can't let him hurt her. Jumping to my feet, I'm across the field and at the driver's door of my truck when see I Uclid at the passenger door. I shake my head at him as he opens it up and jumps in. "No, Man, get out."

"Hell no," he yells. "I'm not lettin' ya face this alone."

He's giving me that 'you better get the fuck in here now' look, and I slam my door shut, cranking my truck to life. Whipping it around, I step on it, leaving a patch of rubber and a cloud of smoke, spitting the gravel of the road out as I head toward the parking lot. The fear, it's creeping in slowly more and more, making my hands shake as I grip the steering wheel.

I only hesitate slightly at the stop signs and lights, making heads turn as I pass the locals all going about their lazy hot day afternoons. Right now the lies can wait to be explained, I just want to make sure she's okay.

"What's the plan?" Uclid says smoothly, his warrior mode kicking in. We never went anywhere without a plan, and I bet he's grooming his new partner for the same tactic. I begin turning down the road connecting the trailer park to town and I let out a ragged breath.

"Make sure she's okay and kick some ass." It's true and in that order. I'll kill him if he's laid a finger on her. Hell, if he even breathed on her, I'll break his arms.

Whipping into the driveway of the park, the back end of my truck fishtails, kicking up the gravel with dust as I see a Harley parked right up against Ellie's porch. I slap my hand on the steering wheel, kicking myself for not making it here sooner. Slamming my foot down on the break, the truck slides and I slam it into park, Uclid being the first to hit the gravel.

*"No! Stop!"* I hear screamed from inside, and it rips me apart as I recognize the sound of a belt striking flesh. Elliot is up the stairs before me and I'm on his heels, wanting to get in there and stop this.

Just as I see Elliot's hand land on the door handle a gunshot rings out, the distinctive pop of a .22, and my heart stops. Covering Uclid's hand, I yank open the door and rush in, unable to say anything.

"You fuckin' bitch," I hear grumbled, and turn my face to see Jake down on his back cradling his leg to his chest with blood running between his fingers. His face is distorted in pain and anger, his pants unbuttoned and his belt lying beside him on the carpet. He turns his eyes toward us and says, "She shot me."

"Good," Uclid offers, making a small smile creep to my lips. But it quickly vanishes as my eyes scan the room, falling on Ellie standing on the linoleum with the gun still pointed at Jake, her arms shaking and her face bruising and bleeding.

Her shirt is torn and I can see the welts rising on her skin through the tears. She's breathing heavy and fast. It looks like she put up a struggle as I spy contents of the kitchen strewn all over the floor.

She's crying, the tears mixing with the blood trickling from the corner of her mouth, and it causes me to move toward her. I stop, instinctively throwing my hands up in front of me in a placating measure when Ellie turns toward me, pointing the gun at me.

"Ellie, it's me," I say softly, trying to break through

that barrier of fear.

Her eye that isn't swelling meets mine. "Bobby?"

~~~~

*Ellie*

"Yeah, it's me," he says, but the fear doesn't fade. The pain is radiating down through my face, seemingly connecting to the welts rising on my back, thighs and butt; caused by Jake's belt. It's all too familiar, this searing heat and roaming hurt, the echo of the leather hitting my bare arms, legs and back ringing through my head.

I don't want to live like this, being the liar, the slut. I don't want to be me any longer.

"Bobby, I'm so sorry," I sob, trying to look at him but my damn eye is almost swollen shut, a victim from the butt of this gun I hold in my hand. He thought he could own me like he had for so many years, but I taught him. Who's the bitch now?

"I know, Sweetheart." His calming voice makes the shaking ease a little, but I don't lower the gun. I said this is going to end. "Now come on, put the gun down and let me help you."

"Don't help that bitch," Jake screams, and I turn on him again, pointing the gun at his face this time instead of his leg. He thought it would be a good idea to pull a gun on me when I was down, but then again he must not have been paying attention when I was taking self-defense classes at the YMCA for the last four months.

"Shut him up," Bobby yells to Elliot, who stalks over, calling Jake names and grabs his shirt collar, dragging him out through the screen door as Jake screams in protest and pain. I follow their path with the gun, my arms trembling with the thought of Jake bouncing to his feet and coming after me again.

I can't let him come after me again. I'd rather die.

"Alright, Sweetheart, it's just me and you." Bobby gives me a smile, easing toward me, and I just shake my head. It'll never be the same. Jake has made sure of that. He made sure he broke me of the chance of finding love again the first time he hit me and I've been stupid enough to think I could overcome it.

"I can't Bobby," I cry, the realization of what I have to do to be really free of Jake pulling down on me like a ton of bricks. He straightens, giving me a questioning look.

"Can't do what, Sweetheart?" he asks, reaching out to me and motioning for me to come to him, but I stay where I am. I can't be near him when I do this.

"Live like this," I say calmly, dropping my one hand from the gun and moving the muzzle up to rest against my temple. The fear playing across his face pulls at my heart, but this is how it has to be. I need to be free of Jake, free of this fear.

"No," he yells, taking a wide step toward me. I move back, holding my hand out to stop him from getting any closer. "No, Ellie, put the gun down. Please." The pleading in his voice kills me.

"I love you, Bobby," I sob, leaning my free shoulder against the wall. "I'm sorry I lied, but I was afraid. I can't be afraid any longer."

"It's okay, Sweetheart, he won't hurt you anymore. He's going to go to jail; I'll make sure of that. Please, just put the gun down. I'll save you from all this." He motions his hand down, wanting me to set it down, but I can't. I can tell he's going to try and lunge for me, his stance giving him away.

"I never asked you to save me," I sob. My head is shaking on its own, the barrel cold against my skin.

This is going to end.

I say, "I'm sorry, Bobby. I love you," and I pull the trigger.

####

# ABOUT THE AUTHOR

Theresa Marguerite Hewitt is a very laid back person; enjoying the simpler things in life more than most sometimes. She grew up in a very, VERY small town in Central New York and she will always be a Redneck Woman. She loves reading, writing, taking long pointless drives and long dusk time walks. Fall and winter are her favorite times of year and she spends more time outside then than in the summer. She loves hearing from fans and isn't above fan-girling on those that show her tons of support. She donates the profits from the Amazon sales of her military series, The Wakefield Romance Series, to various military charities including; Wounded Warrior Project, Red Circle Foundation, Boot Campaign and others. She is addicted to the cheap-Harlequin romances you can pick up in most drug stores and can't go in and out of a store without picking up at least one.
She resides in Buffalo, NY, for now.

THERESA MARGUERITE HEWITT

# EPILOGUE

## BOBBY

*July 4, 2013*

The fireworks just aren't the same. Sure the colors are all here. Red, blue, green, and white; but it's just not the fucking same.

Couples and families are laughing and having a good ol' time down the beach, all looking up with each new boom of color. Not me. I'm sitting here on the edge of the sand, my twelfth beer in hand with anger and hurt overflowing from my chest.

It would be a hell of a lot better if Ellie was sitting here on the beach beside me with her hand in mine, filling that hole that is gaping in my heart. The way she would lay her head on my shoulder and sigh would lift this haze off of my soul in a heartbeat.

The sound of her crying my name as I left her hospital room today is still echoing through my head, even now as the fireworks explode at the shore. It's just that I can't be here any longer; I need to leave.

The twenty-third of June will forever be burned in my mind as the day I almost lost her. Hell, if that asshole Jake wasn't a total idiot and knew how to clean and properly re-assemble his firearm, Ellie would be dead right now. The gun had jammed when she had it pointed to her temple, pulling the trigger just as I lunged for her and when we had hit the linoleum she fell apart in my arms. I have never felt as helpless as I did at that moment; not knowing how to comfort her as she sobbed.

The years of physical, emotional, and mental abuse that she had suffered at the hands of Jake Heart had finally taken its toll, her downfall being triggered by that little show Jake had put on, interrupting our football game. Even now, remembering the pictures and the way he stood there smug as could be, I fist my hands in the sand, surrounded by darkness as the fireworks flash in the sky.

She lied to me. Every day and every night. She lied to me. She *slept* with Garth *and* Brad. She was stripping. It turns my stomach thinking of the disgusting men that ogled over her, throwing money on the stage for her to pick up. Closing my eyes, I try and squeeze out the scenes from those pictures Jake had thrown at me.

Blue-green eyes come into focus as I bring my forehead on my knee, my hands resting on the cold plastic and metal of my prosthetic. Eyes that turn to turquoise in the sun and seem to sparkle as I hear that familiar laugh echo through my mind over the explosion of the firework finale. But no, I won't be seeing those eyes again until we are both ready. Not until we are both healthy enough to love one another the way we should.

I've signed on for a tour of duty with a Private Security Detail, and I'm leaving for Iraq tomorrow morning. Like I said, I need to get away and this is the only way that I know how. I'm a sniper; a trained killer and protector, why not get paid for doing it?

Chad was less than happy when I told him my plans as I quickly packed my duffle bag at his house earlier. He tried to get me to reconsider, saying that I am being rash and immature. Maybe I am, but if I stay here I am bound to go insane.

*"Bobby, please don't leave. I love you. I'm sorry."* Her words run through my head and pull at my heart. The feel of her skin against my lips as I quickly kissed her forehead and basically ran from the hospital seems to be burning across my flesh and I trace its path with my hand, covering my mouth and hardly holding in a yell of frustration and hurt.

Her doctors, along with Rhea's pushing, have convinced Ellie to go into therapy once she's released from the hospital because of her injuries suffered at the hands of her now incarcerated ex-husband. I haven't really talked about that day with Ellie, only spending time in her room when she is asleep and then sneaking out before she wakes up, but I know it will be hard for her. She was broken to the point of no return; run aground I guess you could say.

Looking to my tattooed left arm, I see the pirate ship in the faint illumination from my apartment complex lights and I push myself to my feet, brushing the sand from my shorts. It's like I can feel her fingers tracing the lines of the ship, leaving a tingling feeling in their wake, and I have to shake my arm loose to make it go away. I need the sleep tonight; I have a long day tomorrow.

After pulling off my clothes, I'm thankful for the hot water washing the sting of her kiss from my skin, easing the hurt on my heart for a short while. Leaning my forehead on the tile, I let the water run its way down my torso, closing my eyes and flashes of that day at the pond fly through my head.

I love her, more than words can say. I am in love with her, every fiber of my soul wanting more than anything to tear out of here and storm into her hospital room, wrapping her tight in my arms, never letting her go.

I can't. Not right now at least. We need our space. I need to let her heal on her own, and well, I need to do some soul searching myself. You might say that the desert is the last place I should do the searching, but for right now it's my last option.

Throwing myself down into bed, I cover my eyes with my arm, knowing sleep won't find me anytime soon. "I love you, Ellie Mae," I whisper, a little piece of me hoping that she can hear me, but I know that's an unreasonable prayer.

"I love you, Ellie Mae, and I will never let you go." I roll over and let out a loud sigh, hating myself for leaving, but I know I have to. It's the right move for both of us. "I will never let you go, not in a million years. I'll be back and hopefully we'll be okay."

## TO BE CONTINUED IN BOOK 4 OF THE
## WAKEFIELD ROMANCE SERIES:
# TAKE ME HOME.

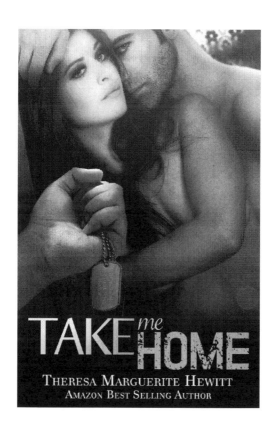

THERESA MARGUERITE HEWITT

# Connect with Theresa Marguerite Hewitt

### Facebook:
https://www.facebook.com/TheresaMargueriteHewittAuthor

### Twitter: @TMarguerite

### Blog: www.theresamargueritehewitt.wordpress.com/

### iMessage:
theresamargueritehewittauthor@gmail.com

### Email: theresamargueritehewittauthor@gmail.com

### Instagram: theresa_marguerite

### Pinterest: Theresa Marguerite

### Smashwords:
https://www.smashwords.com/profile/view/Theres
aMarguerite

# Other Titles By This Author:

Paranormal Romance:

## The Broadus Supernatural Society Series

Book 1: Siofra's Song

Book2: Siofra's Nightmare

Book 3: Siofra's Change

Book 4: Siofra's Fight

Book 5: Rowena's Revenge

Contemporary Romance/Military Romance:

## The Wakefield Romance Series

Book 1: Two Weeks With a SEAL

Book 2: Coming Home

Book 3: I Never Asked You To Save Me

Book 4: Take Me Home

Historical Romance

## The Viking Dreams Series

Book 1: We Roam The Seas

THERESA MARGUERITE HEWITT

51075790R00137

Made in the USA
Middletown, DE
29 June 2019